Someone Else's Valentine

By:

Brooke St. James

Other titles available from Brooke St. James:

So This is Love (Miami Stories #1)
All In (Miami Stories #2)
Something Precious (Miami Stories #3)

The Suite Life (The Family Stone #1)
Feels Like Forever (The Family Stone #2)
Treat You Better (The Family Stone #3)
The Sweetheart of Summer Street (The Family Stone #4)
Out of Nowhere (The Family Stone #5)

Delicate Balance (Blair Brothers #1)
Cherished (Blair Brothers #2)
The Whole Story (Blair Brothers #3)
Dream Chaser (Blair Brothers #4)

Kiss & Tell (Novella) (Tanner Family #0)
Mischief & Mayhem (Tanner Family #1
Reckless & Wild (Tanner Family #2)
Heart & Soul (Tanner Family #3)
Me & Mister Everything (Tanner Family #4)
Through & Through (Tanner Family #5)
Lost & Found (Tanner Family #6)
Sparks & Embers (Tanner Family #7)
Young & Wild (Tanner Family #8)

Easy Does It (Bank Street Stories #1)
The Trouble with Crushes (Bank Street Stories #2)
A King for Christmas (Novella) (A Bank Street Christmas)
Diamonds Are Forever (Bank Street Stories #3)
Secret Rooms and Stolen Kisses (Bank Street Stories #4)
Feels Like Home (Bank Street Stories #5)
Just Like Romeo and Juliet (Bank Street Stories #6)
See You in Seattle (Bank Street Stories #7)
The Sweetest Thing (Bank Street Stories #8)
Back to Bank Street (Bank Street Stories #9)

Split Decision (How to Tame a Heartbreaker #1)
B-Side (How to Tame a Heartbreaker #2)

Cole for Christmas

Somewhere in Seattle (Alexander Family #1)
Wildest Dream (Alexander Family #2)
About to Fall (Alexander Family #3)

Hope for the Best (Morgan Family #1)
Full Circle (Morgan Family #2)
Just for Tonight (Morgan Family #3)

Way Past Mistletoe (Morgan Family #4)
The Wild One (Morgan Family #5)
The Rest is History (Morgan Family #6)
Two is Better Than One (Morgan Family #7)

Twenty-One Roses (The Memphis Players #1)
Someone Else's Valentine (The Memphis Players #2)

Chapter 1

Sasha Faulkner
***
Memphis, Tennessee
Valentine's Day

It was going to be the best night ever. I had been working all day, and now I had an unexpected evening off. I worked part-time at a small chocolate shop on the outskirts of the city. It was normally a quiet establishment, but today was Valentine's Day, which happened to be our busiest day of the year. All day, I had been preparing and selling chocolates like a madwoman.

My plans had been set on working all day and then going to theater rehearsal afterward. I had already told my boyfriend, Nick, that I would not get to see him at all on Valentine's Day. We spent the day together yesterday and exchanged gifts because we knew we wouldn't be together today.

But that was changing now.

Abe, my theater director, surprised the troop with a shortened rehearsal, which never happens. *Who knew he was a softy for Valentine's Day?* Either way, he only kept us for one hour instead of our scheduled four. I had been so busy at work all day that I was absolutely ecstatic when he said we could have the remainder of the night off.

I almost called Nick when I found out, but I decided to surprise him instead. I would go home and shower and then head to his dorm. He would be finished with baseball practice, and his only plans were to hang out with his roommates, so I knew he'd be on campus.

I took a shower and got dressed. My dark brown hair hung in wild curls just below my shoulders. I washed it yesterday, and it was still in good shape in spite of work, so I kept it dry in the shower. I left it down, quickly situating it so that it framed my face and looked the best it could in a limited amount of time. I performed a practiced routine with my hair and makeup, but I made it happen quickly so that I could get over to Nick's. In no time at all, I was dressed up in my impromptu Valentine's Day outfit—my favorite jeans and a light pink top with ruffles.

It was a little after seven when I parked on campus and made my way into his dorm. He and his brother, William, had an apartment-style dorm that they shared with four other guys from the baseball team. There was a common living area with couches, a television, and a kitchen with a dining room. On the right, past the living room, there was a hallway with three bedrooms and a large, shared bathroom area. And on the left was a mirror image, three more bedrooms, and another shared bathroom.

I had lived in the dorms at my college during my freshman and sophomore years, and they were nowhere near as nice as these. All of the guys had their own, private bedroom, and they only had to share a bathroom with two other guys. This building was supposed to be dorms for upperclassmen, but some athletes had special privileges associated with their scholarships.

Nick was an excellent second baseman, and he was in college on a full scholarship. We started dating during his off-season, and so I hadn't yet seen him play in an official game. I had been to tons of practices, though, and I watched some scrimmages. I knew he was good. I loved baseball, and Nick appreciated that about me. He and I had been together for six months, so today was our first Valentine's Day together.

I was brimming with excitement to surprise him. Most of Nick's friends had girlfriends, so he had nothing to do tonight. He had texted to let me know that after practice, he was staying at the apartment, doing nothing but being bored. I was excited to surprise him. I knocked on the apartment door, but no one answered, so I walked inside.

I didn't see anyone in the common area when I came inside, which was rare. Six guys lived here, and they were all popular, so there were usually multiple people in the living room. I half-expected

Nick himself to be in there, or maybe even his brother. It was odd that the place was so empty.

Nick and William lived at opposite ends of the apartment, but they were always together, and I hung out socially with William and his girlfriend all the time. I called out, looking for them.

"Nick?" I said, hollering as I came into the living room. "Hellooo?"

I walked toward Nick's room, crossing the living area and then the kitchen. All three doors at the end of the hallway were closed, and I heard music coming from what sounded like two of them.

I was standing in the hallway near the communal bathroom when I heard a door open and close on the other side of the apartment. I glanced over my shoulder to find that William, Nick's big brother, was there. I caught a glimpse of the tattoo on his back as he crossed from the bathroom to his bedroom. He was wearing a towel around his waist and he opened his bedroom door without even looking my way.

I started to yell at him with a greeting, but he was all the way across the apartment, so I decided to stay on track and head to Nick's room. I was about to turn away from William, but then I saw movement. William glanced my way and noticed me standing there. I watched, from a distance, as his face worked to understand who he was seeing.

"Hey, Will," I said, smiling big and calling to him from across the way. I wasn’t shocked by his lack of clothing. I had been in this room a lot, and I had seen more than a few of the guys with nothing but a towel on.

William gave me a little wave.

I had brought Nick a few chocolates from work, and I balanced them in one hand so I could wave back at his brother. William turned to go into his room, and I turned to refocus on finding my boyfriend.

I had only taken a step toward Nick's door when I heard a low, tumbling sound happening behind me. It was the sound of footfall. It was swift, and it quickly grew louder. I had no idea what the sound was at first, and by the time I figured it out, he was right on top of me. I turned and gasped, bracing myself stiffly because William had run across the entire apartment and was suddenly right next to me. He rushed me, almost knocking me over.

I took an unsteady step, gaining my balance and getting a grip on the chocolates as William reached out to help steady me. He stared directly at me, gazing at me intensely.

"What are you doing here, Sasha? We thought you had to work, or theater. What are you doing? Nick's not even here."

I glanced in the direction of Nick's door. "Oh, he's not? Where is he? I was trying to surprise him. I got off of rehearsal early, and I thought he was here, so I was… why is his stereo on?" I asked, pausing and looking at William. At first, I was asking just because I thought it was curious, and then in those seconds, it hit me that William might be lying to me. I was innocent, so I smiled at him, assuming that if he was lying about anything, it was because Nick wanted to surprise me.

"Nick left the radio on when he left, but he's not here. He's gone." William took my shoulders and physically turned me around, pointing me toward the door, but I resisted, stopping in my tracks and turning to look at him since physically pushing me out of a room was not something he normally did. I had hugged William before, but he usually didn't take me by the shoulders and start steering me around like a child.

"If he's not here, I'll just leave his chocolates in his room," I said, moving to step around him.

William blocked me.

He stepped to the side, physically preventing me from getting past him.

I made eye contact with him.

I stepped to the other side, and he blocked me again.

"Nick wouldn't care if I opened his door and left some chocolate on his dresser."

William made a face at me that was regretful, sorrowful. He pitied me, and in those seconds, the truth sank in.

Oh, gosh. This was bad, wasn't it?

A wave of embarrassment crashed over me.

I instantly felt suffocated by humiliation.

I couldn't find words.

I couldn't breathe.

I stuttered when I began to speak. "I-I-I'm going in there to leave this chocolate," I said slowly, blinking at William as tears rose to my eyes.

"Really, Sasha. Don't. Nick's not here. You need to leave. If you want to leave the chocolate, leave it over there, in the fridge."

"Why are you doing this, William?"

"Because, I like you, Sasha. Just go. We have naked guys in this house. Girls aren't supposed to be allowed up here. You can go try to call Nick from your car."

He was pushing me again, steering me, causing me to walk in front of him. We took steps, through the kitchen, through the living room, and to the door. He pushed me toward it, and I took a step and then turned to stare back at him like I couldn't believe what he was doing.

"What is wrong with you, William?"

"I'm sorry, Sasha." He shook his head when he said it. And there it was again… that look of genuine regret—pity. "Just go for now, and try to call Nick later."

I put my hand on the doorknob in order to open it and leave, but I looked at William. I opened my mouth to speak, but I couldn't get the words out. I obviously wanted to know if there was another girl in Nick's room. I almost came right out and asked it. The phrase, *"is there another girl in Nick's room?"*

echoed in my mind, but I could not get the words to come out of my mouth.

"I'm sorry," he said again when I didn't speak.

And just like that, he turned and walked away. I watched as William retreated, heading down the hallway, toward his own room.

Those seconds were so confusing that it was excruciating. Part of me wanted to go back to Nick's room, part of me wanted to run to my car, and part of me wanted to stay right there in the living room until everything got figured out. I had several thoughts going on at one time, and all I did was turn and walk numbly out of the door.

I left the chocolate on the floor. I just absentmindedly turned and dropped the bag at my feet as I walked out of their apartment and into the main dorm hallway.

I saw someone I recognized on the way to my car—it was one of the players from the team—one of Nick's friends. He waved at me, and I waved back, but I was in no shape to talk to anyone, so I kept moving, kept walking, and kept my head down.

By the time I made it to my car, I came to terms with the fact that my boyfriend was probably cheating on me. The problem was that I should have stayed in that apartment and gotten proof. As it stood, there was just no way for me to know. *Of course, he would deny it if I asked him, and what was I to make of all this information?* William's reaction to me being at the house coupled with the fact that there was music coming from Nick's room made me feel eighty percent sure that I was being cheated on at this very moment.

I was in love with Nick, and this whole thing was so unexpected and from out of nowhere that I felt lightheaded. I sat in my car with my head in my hands, trying to get myself together and plan my next move.

You should go back up there.

You don't want to see what's happening.

You need to see what's happening.

William said Nick was gone, and his truck was there, in the parking lot. I looked at it.

You know what's happening.

No, you really don't.

He could be gone with a friend.

You'll never be sure if you don't go up there and find out.

You can't go back up there.

William has already kicked you out.

But I knew I could go back, and I seriously contemplated it.

I sat there for the next five minutes trying to work up the nerve to go into that apartment and open Nick's door. I felt like a stalker for sitting in front of his building, which was completely outrageous since I was his girlfriend and had every right to be there.

I called Nick from the parking lot, but he didn't pick up. I texted him, telling him to text me back right when he got the message.

I imagined myself going up to their apartment again. I tried to see the whole thing in my mind's eye. I imagined banging on his bedroom door and demanding that he come out, or opening the door myself and finding the two of them there, half-naked and panting with lipstick all over their faces.

I didn't realize I was crying until I looked down at my hands and saw some of my mascara on them. Pulled down the visor and looked into the mirror, blinking as I stared at the reflection. My eyes were red and full of tears. My mascara was running. Surely if I went upstairs like this, I would look like a crazy person.

I had William's number and I called him. He did not pick up, so I called him again. He didn't pick up that time either, so I texted him.

Me:

William, it's Sasha. I assume by the way you acted that Nick is cheating on me. I assume someone was in that room with him. Another girl. Please don't let him make a fool out of me. Just tell me the truth. Is Nick cheating on me?

I pressed send, and then I immediately typed another text and sent it as well.

Me:

If you tell me the truth, I'll leave and not come back up there to see for myself.

I sat there, staring at my phone, waiting for some kind of answer.

A few minutes passed, and I was about to get out of my car and go up there, but I heard a notification on my phone.

It was a text from William.

William:
Just leave and go your separate ways.

That was all it said.

I stared down at it.

I blinked, and more tears fell.

William was telling me that my suspicions were true. He was saying that Nick was cheating on me.

Chapter 2

I couldn't let it go.

It wasn't exactly clear what William was saying in that text, and I wasn't willing to leave campus without knowing for sure.

I drove out of the parking lot, and I looped around one block, crying, sweating, and freaking out as I decided what to do next. I went back there and parked in a different location where I could still see the entrance to his building.

None of this seemed abnormal to me at the time. I was so broken emotionally that parking and watching the front of Nick's building felt like a completely logical thing for me to do right then.

For the next hour, I sat there in a daze, watching the door and contemplating whether or not I wanted to go back inside. The whole time, I was hoping I would see him come back with a friend.

The door opened lots of times with people coming and going, and never was it Nick.

But then it happened. The door flung open, and I watched as two people walked outside. I could tell one of them was Nick, even from a distance. He was with a girl—someone I recognized.

William's girlfriend was a cheerleader, and this girl was one of her friends from the squad. She was sporty and cute, and her body was perfect.

I felt nauseous. My stomach was tied in knots. They walked next to each other, Nick smiling as he looked her way. They didn't hold hands, but I knew what Nick looked like when he wanted to impress a girl, and he was doing it right then. He had looked at me that way.

My vision blurred as my eyes filled with tears, but I blinked so that I could focus on them. I knew I needed to see this.

Oh, gosh, did I?

I should've left already. I should have believed William when he told me to leave. But now I had proof. I made myself stay and see the proof, and there it was, right in front of me.

He walked her to her car, and I lost sight of them for what must've been three minutes. I was just about to drive away, heading out the other direction when I saw Nick again.

He came into my line of vision, heading into the building. I watched as he turned and waved to her when she drove off. He leaned to the left and slapped playfully at a branch, catching some of it in his hand. He tossed up something, maybe an acorn, and hit it with his hand like he was batting a ball.

He was in a great mood, being playful, jumping up the steps, taking them two at a time.

Naomi was her name.

I had seen her around.

Nick hesitated near the door, smiling as he checked his phone. He leaned against the wall, staring down at it with a smile on his face.

I should've driven away, but I watched him, transfixed.

It was a complete shock to me when my phone rang. It was sitting in the console next to me, and I glanced down at it to find that it was Nick calling.

He held his phone to his ear, listening, waiting for me to pick up.

It was difficult to work past the emotion and the nausea, but I did it. I pressed the green button to answer the call, and I cleared my throat, fixing my voice. I closed my eyes so that I could do my very best at sounding like I was unaffected.

"Hello?" I said, innocently.

"Hey, Sash, what are you doing?"

"Nothing," I said, again trying to sound happy and control my shaky voice. "What are you doing?" I added. "I went by your apartment earlier. I left chocolate. William made me leave. He said you weren't home."

I got the words out, thank goodness.

"Oh, I know, he texted me and said you came by. But I wasn't home. I'm back now, though. I just pulled up a second ago. I'm about to walk into my apartment."

I had been watching him as he spoke. He started walking into his apartment building as he told me he was going inside, as if following through with that truth would somehow make any of this better.

"Oh, cool, so you're just getting back to the dorms?" I asked.

"Yeah, why, do you want to come over? What happened? Did you get off of rehearsal early?"

"Yeah. I came over earlier. I left chocolates for Valentine's Day."

Nick let out a little laugh, sounding casual. "I hope my roommates didn't eat them already."

"Your door was closed, and your stereo was on."

"What?"

"And William basically threw me out of the apartment. He panicked when he saw me."

"What, Sasha? What are you talking about?"

"Why are you so defensive?" I asked.

"I'm not. I just don't even know what you're talking about right now. This is coming out of left field. I just pulled up at my dorm, like, thirty seconds ago. I have no idea what's going on. I've been at my parents' house since practice let out. I went to eat over there."

"Your truck was at the dorms."

"Because Cameron came with me. He drove."

The lies caused me physical pain. Hearing him blatantly lie like that confirmed that he was hiding the other girl, and it also somehow instantly killed any feelings I had for Nick. It was like a switch had turned off. I lost all respect for him, and instantly I began mourning that fact.

My heart was crushed.

I could hardly think straight.

"Keep the chocolate, but we're done, Nick. Have fun with the other girl."

"What? Sasha? What are you saying? Don't be stupid," he said playfully, acting coy.

"I was stupid. I can't believe how stupid I was. I actually loved you, Nick."

I pictured the sight of perky Naomi in her perfect little short shorts, bouncing around like a happy little puppy.

"I love you, too!" Nick insisted casually. "What are you even talking about?" He was still smiling. I could hear it in his voice.

"Just stop it. Naomi. I saw her. I saw you with her. Just stop lying, Nick. We're through. I'm hanging up now."

I hung up the phone, and that was it.

Nothing happened.

I don't know what I expected, but it didn’t happen. I sat there in my car, and nothing happened at all.

The silence was deafening. I could feel my heart pounding in my stomach. I was still nauseated and had a bad taste in my mouth.

I turned on my car and dazedly headed home.

The silence followed me as I drove.

I did not turn on the stereo, and no one called.

I was all alone, just me and God.

That was the thing. I had thought God was involved in me dating Nick. Everything had been so perfect. I loved him, and honestly thought he loved me. I thought our lives were supposed to be intertwined. I had no idea how I could be so blind. I felt betrayed, not only by Nick, but by William and everyone else who saw them together.

How long had it been going on?

My thoughts were spiraling out of control, and I hardly remembered driving. I didn't even know how I came to be at my apartment.

My roommates were home, but neither of them were in the living room when I went through there. I was relieved because I would not have been able to speak to them, anyway.

This was a crusher.

For the last six months, I had been so all-in with Nick that I had begun to build a life and plans for a future with him. His sister was one of my best friends, for crying out loud. We had lived near their family when we were kids, and I had a crush on him from a distance. He was younger than me, and he and William were always athletes and in a totally different world than my brother. It wasn't until recently when I had the chance to get to know Nick better that we figured out we had a lot in common.

We had been inseparable for months.

My actual life plans had been altered because of him, and I felt like a fool. I was a fool. How could I have been so serious about something when he was clearly so casual?

It was not a good evening. I spent most of it in my room. Nick never tried to call, which somehow made it more painful. I would have denied him if he did call, but he didn't even try. His sister, Bailey, didn't call me either.

I had all sorts of thoughts that evening and into the next morning. I was supposed to go to class at 8am, and I skipped it by emailing the professor and telling him I wasn't feeling well. It was not a lie.

By the afternoon, when neither Nick nor Bailey had yet called me, I was convinced Nick had said something to turn his family against me.

Losing Bailey's friendship was almost as gut-wrenching as losing Nick, and I was in a bad place all day.

None of my friends or family knew this had happened, and my phone was eerily quiet. I had centered my life so fully on Nick lately that I hadn't even realized how quiet my existence would be without him. Thankfully, I had no play rehearsal that night, because there was no way I could go function in that world.

I had work scheduled that afternoon, though, and I was considering going. It was the day after Valentine's Day, and I knew the store would be dead.

I was only with one other woman on the schedule, and she was quiet and preoccupied, so I knew I could get away with just spacing out and doing busy work. Plus, it would do me some good to get out of my apartment.

I went to work at two o'clock, and I was supposed to leave at six. Sharon was supposed to stay until eight so she could close, but I knew how to do it, so I offered to let her leave. Sharon happily took me up on it.

Our little chocolate shop was mostly abandoned today, anyway. Valentine's Day was one of our few busy days of the year. We had some molds and machines where people could see some of our production line, and it was a popular place for tourists to go… in 1965, maybe.

We were still technically a Memphis classic, and people did still come out here to see us make chocolate but not at six o'clock in the evening—and especially not on the day after Valentine's Day.

All afternoon, we only had a handful of customers, and there hadn't been a single one in over an hour. Sharon went home, leaving me with nothing but a reminder to count the register and lock up.

I shed a few tears when she left.

I checked my phone and I still had no calls from Nick or Bailey. I had no calls from anyone, not even my brother or my parents. The silence made me sad, and I cried.

I decided to clean the floors. I did it so that I could have an excuse to do something besides wallow in my own self-pity. I put on my headphones and a vintage rock playlist, and the instant the music hit my ears, I began dancing. I put on some dark sunglasses to hide myself from the world, and I went to work, sweeping, mopping, singing, and dancing, doing anything to distract myself from the pain of heartache. I cried some, but I worked through it, telling myself I'd be all right.

I was in the middle of mopping when a really cool song came on. My playlist had moved on to recommended songs, and it was one I didn't usually hear. It made me smile, even from the first few notes. My eyes were still burning, and my face hurt and felt like it was cracking when I smiled. The song did that to me—made me smile.

It was a song I had heard before, but I didn't know who sang it. It had a quirky beginning that was just my style, and I posed with the mop in my hand and danced and listened to the words.

I started it over, and caught it again, from the beginning, loving that guitar.

I danced through the entire intro.

Darling you've got to let me know,
Should I stay or should I go?
If you say that you are mine,
I'll be here till the end of time.
So you've got to let me know,
Should I stay or should I go?

It's always tease, tease, tease,

You're happy when I'm on my knees.
One day is fine the next is black,
So, if you want me off your back.
Well, come on and let me know,
Should I stay or should I go?

The lyrics could have crushed me, but they did the opposite—they made me feel like I was in control, like I was the one calling the shots. Not only that, but the beat itself made me feel confident and happy at the most unexpected time.

The chorus went into singing about how if I go there will be trouble and if I stay there would be double... and I was f-e-e-l-i-n-g it. Somehow this song made me feel confident about my life moving forward—like there was a chance I might not die from the heartache of all this.

I danced, feeling the beat and moving in perfectly timed, confident movements. I had choreographed segments stored in my muscle memory from doing previous musicals on stage, and I applied them to this dance. I turned up the volume and closed my eyes, digging every last note of the music, smiling and knowing that my life would go on. I was strong enough to overcome this.

When it finished, I started the same song one more time. Dancing seemed to help. I still didn't understand why God would let this happen to me. I knew I trusted Him, but I didn't know where He was at the moment. The song helped me find some confidence. Dancing helped me remember I had strength inside of me. Maybe the old church adage was true—maybe there was something to trading worry for praise.

Just then, I heard a clapping noise that wasn't part of the song, and I gasped and almost dropped the mop when I looked up and saw a person standing right there in the store with me.

It was a small store, and he was only a few feet away. He had on a baseball cap, and he was young and handsome, and there was just no way I could look at his face. It was a good thing I had on gigantic, dark sunglasses. I stared at his shirt and not his face.

"I'm so sorry. I didn't see you come in. Welcome to Kramer's," I said, taking off my headphones.

Chapter 3

Warren Manning

Alt-Country/Soul singer,
Elvis fan,
rebel at heart

"Pull over right here," Warren said. "Just pull into this parking lot, and we'll find it."

"We don't have time, Warren. Becky's hassling us, and as it stands, you're only getting like four hours of sleep before you get on a plane in the morning."

"Pull over, Jared," was all Warren replied.

Jared pulled over. He had been Warren's best friend for years, and he knew when Warren was serious.

"I might've left it at the Ernestine & Hazel's." Warren continued. He was referring to the blues club where he had just surprised fans by performing not one but *three* songs during a dinner set with the house band. It was almost a madhouse by the end of it—people had called their friends.

Jared groaned, sounding perturbed at the thought of going back there. "We shouldn't have been there for that long in the first place. It was lucky we got out before your truck got blocked. And now we have to go back?"

"I’m not sure that I left it. But I need to get out so I can look under here and see for sure. I could've sworn I had it in my pocket when we got in."

Jared pulled into a parking lot that was situated next to a small place called Kramer's Chocolates. Warren climbed out of the passenger's side, and Jared did the same thing, getting out of the driver's side and beginning to look around the floorboard of the truck with a determined stare.

"Oh, I see it," Warren said peering under the seat. He got a glimpse of the corner of his phone case, and he knew it was down there in the worst spot possible. He reached his hand under the seat but he couldn't touch it. He tried sliding his hand down the 'crack of doom', and he still couldn't reach it.

"Try the backseat," he said to Jared, knowing his friend was willing to help. Jared went around to the backseat and attempted to reach the phone from the backside of the passenger's seat.

He had no luck. He could see the device but he could not reach it.

"Let's just leave it," Jared said when he saw neither of them were having luck. "We see where it is. We know it's not lost. We can get it out of there when we get back to Nashville."

"No, Jared. We have three hours on the road. I'm getting my phone. We'll figure it out, just give me a second."

"Where are you going?" Jared asked when he heard the door close.

"I'm going in this store to see if they have a chopstick or anything. All I need is something I can push it with, then I could grab it from under the seat."

"It's a chocolate store, not a sushi bar. They're not going to have a chopstick. They're probably not even open."

"I'll be right back. Just chill for a second. I want some chocolate for the road, anyway."

Warren saw a small hatchback car parked in the lot, and the lights were on in the store, but he honestly didn't know if the place was open.

He walked along the sidewalk, toward the door. There was a large window next to the front door and Warren looked inside before he walked in. A woman was dancing with a mop in her hand. She had a curly brown ponytail high on her head with a pair of oversized headphones and sunglasses.

Warren was almost certain that the door would be locked when he tried to open it. He thought they were closed since the cleaning person was here and no one else. It was unlocked, though, and Warren watched in stunned amazement as she continued to dance even after he opened it. He wore a huge grin because he loved her moves. He loved how she looked. She was short and just curvy enough to make his heart race.

She had on oversized, dark sunglasses and she was totally oblivious to his arrival, even after he called out to her and waved. She either had her eyes closed or she was blind because Warren made himself obvious.

Finally, he put himself only a few feet from her and then clapped a couple of times. That got her. She heard him, and when she opened her eyes, she gasped and jumped back, nearly dropping her mop.

"Oh, I'm so sorry. I didn't see you come in," she said. "Welcome to Kramer's." She took off her headphones and rested them around her neck, but the dark sunglasses remained in place.

"Thank you," he said.

She went behind the counter to put up the mop and wash her hands, assuming he was there to look at chocolate.

"Let me know when you're ready," she said, not paying attention to him.

"Oh, you're open?"

"Yes, we're open. We're just slow so, I… was cleaning. I'm sorry I didn't see you come in."

Warren was famous enough that people often recognized him when he went out in public. He didn't have on his trusty Chicago Cubs baseball cap, but he had on a different cap, and he was easily recognizable with his longish hair. His eyes were also a rare shade of blue. Quite simply, he was a recognizable guy, and most young women knew who he was, at least most young women in rural Tennessee.

Warren was a Nashville baby. His mom had aspired to be a country star herself. She had left his dad in Texas and gone to Nashville when Warren was a baby. He grew up there, going to honky-tonks as a toddler. He had been singing all his life, but it wasn't until a few years ago that he gained mainstream popularity.

This girl did not care who he was. She was preoccupied and had hardly turned his way since he had been in the building. She had on baggy grey sweatpants with a fitted dark green polo shirt that had Kramer's Chocolates embroidered on the chest. She wore two different shoes, one pink Converse and one purple one, and those sunglasses were huge and dark. They were covering half of her face. He thought she was probably pretty under there.

"Hey, this is completely unorthodox thing for me to ask, but I didn't originally come in here for chocolate. I dropped my phone in the crack of my truck and we pulled over because I can't reach it. We're on our way back to Nashville. Your hands are smaller than mine. Would you come out to the parking lot and help me?"

"Sure," she agreed calmly, as if she didn't have a care in the world. She dried her hands after washing them and started toward the door, looking like she was going to go outside without any questions.

"Do you normally dance when you work?" he asked as he reached for the door.

She let out a little laugh as he opened it. "No. I've been known to dance, but not here. We're just dead tonight. I'm definitely more prone to dance than to follow a strange guy out to the parking lot."

"I'm not strange at all," he said defensively. "My phone fell into the crack, and I need someone with small hands to reach it, that's all. Or a chopstick—something I could poke it with. I have to drive back to Nashville, and didn't want to leave it down there."

But she had stopped walking before Warren finished talking. He turned to look at her curiously, and she dug in her pocket. She smiled as she came up with a pencil.

"Here you go," she said. "Is that all you need?" She stood still like she was no longer planning on following him. They could see his truck from here—it was a quarter-of-a-million-dollar vehicle with all the bells and whistles, and she didn't give it a second look.

"Yeah, I guess it is," he said, surprised.

"Great. There you go. Have a safe trip," she announced in a tone of goodbye.

She turned to head back inside without another word, and Warren could do nothing but stare at her. He turned and followed her by instinct. It was dark outside, and *what the heck were these dark sunglasses about?* Warren was intrigued by this girl. She was different. Also, her dancing was absolutely adorable and Warren felt his heart beat faster when he remembered how she was moving before she noticed him. She had been smiling and making subtle faces as she moved, and Warren was so intrigued that he followed her even though he knew he should take the pencil and leave.

"What are you doing?" she asked when she noticed that he was following her.

"I'm going back inside to get some chocolate."

"You said you didn't come for chocolate."

"I said that I originally came for my phone, but now that I've been inside and smelled the chocolate, I can hardly resist."

She glanced his way while he held the door, but it was barely a glance.

"What's your name?" he asked.

"Sasha."

"That's a cool name. Is it spelled just like it sounds? S-A-S-H-A?"

"Yes, why?" she asked hesitating.

He shrugged. "I don't know. I was just curious."

"Yes. S-A-S-H-A. Take your time looking around. We don't close for another thirty minutes. Let me know when you decide on something." She took off, walking toward the back, and Warren's curiosity kicked in. She had been only inches from his face, and he could tell she was not looking at him. He could not see her eyes behind those sunglasses, but he knew they weren't focused on him.

"What's with the sunglasses?" he asked.

"What if I'm blind?"

"Are you?"

"No. But what if I was? That would've been weird that you said 'what's with the sunglasses'? You don't know what's going on with me. I might have had my eyes dilated today."

"Did you?"

"No. But you didn't know that."

"Well, I'm sorry for saying it like that but it's dark outside, and they're really big and black, and I wish I knew what your face looked like, that's all."

She let out a little laugh. "No, you don't. I look horrible right now. That's exactly what's with the sunglasses."

"What do you mean you look horrible? Are you talking about wearing no makeup?"

"Yes, I'm talking about my lack of makeup."

He could tell she was just saying that to appease him, but he didn't know what to make of her. This whole situation made him feel intrigued.

"No one's in here to look at you," he said. "And I certainly don't care if you have on makeup."

She moved, and Warren watched as she reached up and took off her sunglasses. Her eyes were puffy and swollen and it was one hundred percent obvious that she had been crying. Warren had seen a lot of crying women in his day. This was a look of a face after someone had shed a lot of tears.

"It's not just about makeup," she admitted. "I look like a big blubbering mess under here."

"Are you okay?" he asked, calmly and sincerely. "I'm sorry, Sasha. I feel bad for mentioning the sunglasses."

She put them back on. "It's fine, really."

"Do you need help? Any help? I could help you."

"No, I was just having a moment in here where I sort of let it all out. I was in here by myself, and I just had my heart broken yesterday, so I was taking a minute to just be here in my feelings." She paused briefly, but then took a breath and continued. "It was amazing, though, because after I cried, a song came on, and… you know what? It's just wonderful how music works. Music is magic. I heard that song, as silly as it was, and I, I danced to it. And somehow, in those six minutes while that song was playing, something happened in my heart. I realized I was okay. I know it sounds silly, but a few minutes ago, I was crying like a baby, and somehow a song just fixed it. So yes, my face looks like this from earlier, but I'm totally better now. I know that's weird of me to say, but it's true. I'm good now."

"What song was it?" he asked, hoping it was one of his.

"I don't even know who sings it."

"Is it country?"

"No," she said with a little laugh, like she would never listen to country music. "Maybe it's the Rolling Stones. I'm not sure."

"Is it an old song?"

"Yes, and I've heard it before, I just don't know who sings it."

"How does it go?"

"*Should I stay or should I go now?*" She sang the tune in a deep voice with a slight British edge to her accent. She did not care that she was being silly, and Warren smiled.

"That's not The Stones, that's, The Clash, I think. Check and see. Look at your phone."

She took out her phone.

Warren watched her.

"Yeah, you're right. They're called The Clash. I don't know them. It was just on a recommended playlist."

"And that was the song that helped you out of your funk?"

"Yeah, crazy, I know. Music is just so much more than songs, though. It gets in your heart. It can change you from the inside."

"You don't have to convince me of that," he said. "I love music."

"Amen, brother," she said. She reached over the counter to high-five him.

Warren felt inspired by this woman. He wanted to write a song about this interaction, about the fact that she was dancing away a broken heart.

He hated whoever had done that to her.

Who could break her heart?

She was so sweet that such an act seemed cruel. She had her sunglasses back on by now, and she continued to purposefully avoid eye contact with Warren. Even when she gave him a high-five she was smiling and looking in a different direction. He wondered if it was because she had been hurt. He thought she had a pure heart, and he was sad that someone had broken it.

Chapter 4

Sasha Faulkner

"You're better off without that guy," the stranger said after a minute. He was being nice, trying to make me feel better.

"Thank you," I said, still refusing to look directly at him.

"I'll take whatever chocolate you want to put in a box for me," he said. "And I don't care how much it costs," he added. "Just make me an assortment for the road."

I smiled and began the routine of putting on gloves and shaping a large box. I wasn't in the mood to overthink things, and I went to work putting bits of chocolates in a box, and creating what was basically our most popular mixed specialty box.

"Are you sure you're okay?" he asked.

"Yes. I'm just mad at myself for wasting so much time on a guy. I neglected my school work, and I didn't make plans for my own life because I was encouraging him and supporting him—depending on his plans. His sister is one of my… you know what? It doesn't matter. I'll figure it out with my friends." I knew I had already said too much, and I gave him a forced smile. "I really do feel better now. I'm just sporting the sunglasses for fun at this point. This is going to be forty or fifty dollars for this box. Is that okay? I could put some back."

"It's not too much. Put some of those square things in there. What are those?"

"Those are my favorites," I said.

"Why didn't you give them to me in the first place?"

I started to open my mouth to defend myself and say something about the classic assortment, but then I stopped. "Because I didn't think about it," I said, still not looking at him "How many of these?"

"Just give me what you have left."

"There's ten of them here."

"That's fine."

"They're two-sixty-five a piece."

"That's okay, too. You know what? Can you put some of these in a separate box?"

"Sure."

"I always have people at my house," he said.

I smiled at him but I didn't ask about all the people. I had no reason to care where these chocolates were going. I put some extras into a small box.

"Anything else?"

"Can you put a few more in each of those?"

"Of course," I said, and I continued to work.

"Tell me something about yourself, Sasha."

"I like sudoku. I'm a math girl. I tutor some kids. I do musical theater, too."

"Whoa. I didn't know those two things would mix."

"I'm not super serious about it—either of them. I do community theater as a hobby. I used to do it more, but now it's just one or two shows a year. That's what the dancing was about. Most of that stuff you witnessed earlier was from a musical. I'm not a star or anything. I'm rarely one of the mains. I'm okay, I can get by, but theater's not my life goal or anything."

I closed the boxes and went to the register.

"That's so interesting. I walk into a chocolate shop and find someone who does musical theater."

"I'm also a student. I'm a junior in college."

"Studying what?"

"Accounting. That's where the math comes in."

I glanced at him to find that he was looking at me. He lifted his arm up and scratched his head in a confused, curious gesture as he regarded me.

"Why are you so surprised?" I asked.

"Because you have on mismatched shoes. I wouldn't peg you as an accountant."

I pressed buttons on the cash register, ringing him up as I absentmindedly spoke. "Well, I'm not quite sure what I think of accounting, either. It's just a job. I like numbers, and I'm usually good at school, but I'm behind right now. I missed a lot last semester, and this one. I need to get back into it. I've got finals coming up." I paused and hit the button to get his total. "Speaking of accounting, your chocolate comes to seventy-eight-twenty-five. Is that okay? I threw in a couple for free."

"It's fine. I can pay whatever." He handed me his card, and I ran it.

He seemed like a really sincere guy, but I kept my gaze shifted away from him and went through the motions of finishing the sale at a cordial distance. I bagged the boxes, putting the smaller one neatly on top of the larger one.

"Thank you," I said, handing him the bag. "I hope you have a safe trip back to Nashville."

"This one's for you," he said.

He reached inside, and I glanced his way to find that he was standing there with the smaller box.

"I can't take that," I said, meeting his eyes. I only held the contact for a second because they were white-hot ice-blue eyes—the kind that made women weak in the knees. "I can't," I repeated when I looked away. "Those are for you."

"No, they're not. I bought them for you."

He was holding the box in the air, and he nudged it toward me. I took it out of his hand reluctantly.

"Are you sure?" I said.

"I'm definitely sure," he said. "Please. I want you to have it."

"Thank you," I said, glancing at him with a look of thankful shock. I was *mostly* glancing at him. I couldn't make myself look directly into his devastating baby blues, but I vaguely looked in his direction—near his ear, and the empty areas of his cheek and jaw. It didn't matter where I focused because I had on sunglasses, anyway.

"I really liked meeting you, Sasha."

"I liked meeting you too," I said, pretending I was not at all embarrassed by being caught dancing earlier. "Thank you again for these." I almost told him that nobody had ever bought me chocolate before, but I didn't say it.

"You're welcome," he said. "Bye, Sasha."

He walked slowly toward the door, turning and regarding me before he walked out.

"Bye."

I normally didn't talk to customers like this, and it made me feel so odd. I wouldn't say it was awkward, but there was definitely a little something more to what we had than a regular customer-cashier encounter. He had bought me chocolate, for goodness sake. Maybe I was just overthinking it because of the chocolate. I was still out of it because of Nick, anyway.

I waved at the handsome stranger and smiled to reiterate our goodbye.

"I'm glad you're feeling better. And my name is Warren, by the way."

"Oh, hey, Warren. I am feeling better. You're so nice. Thanks again for the chocolates."

"Thanks for being open, and for the pencil." He gestured to it. It was behind his ear, and I caught sight of his face when I looked at where he was pointing. Goodness. The baseball cap. I loved it when guys wore those, and I thought it would remind me of Nick, but this man looked nothing like Nick. He was a heart-stopper. His face was all sharp angles with baby-smooth skin. He had some light dusting of facial hair, and it worked on him. He turned, and I watched as he walked out of the door and then down the sidewalk and out of my life.

To get to Nashville, he would have to take a right out of the parking lot. I sat there, watching the window and knowing I would never see him again. I was floored that he gave me so much chocolate. *Who does something like that?* I took one out and ate it right there, blinking and thinking about the exchange.

I was not over Nick or the way he hurt me—but the song, followed by the unexpected gift from a gorgeous stranger was such a sweet ending to an otherwise horrible day. I knew no one would come into the store during these last few minutes we were open, so I used the free time and my newfound ounce of courage to text my good friend, Bailey, Nick's sister.

She was currently living in California, finishing her degree. In spite of her geographical location, she and I had gotten even closer since Nick and I got together. That fact made this text a difficult one for me. I probably should have called, but I sent a text instead.

Me:

Hey, I'm sorry for not calling sooner, but I didn't know how I'd ever say this to you and be able to hold it together. Nick and I broke up. I love you, and I will be so devastated if this changes anything between me and you. I'm sorry. I love you.

I sent it, and a few seconds later, my phone rang.

It was, of course, Bailey.

I let out a nervous sigh as I pressed the button to answer it.

"What happened?" was the first thing she said when I answered the phone.

"I'm not going to go into details because I'm all cried out, but he cheated on me."

"No, he did not."

"Yes, he did."

"I'm so sorry, Sasha. Do you know for sure?"

"I don't know what all happened, but, yes. And William knew about it. He was at the dorm, basically guarding the door, when I walked in."

"Did you catch Nicholas with someone else?"

"Yes, I did. I recognized her and everything. It sucks so bad, Bailey. I can't even…" I hesitated, begging myself to keep it together and remember the confidence I found during that song. I tried, in those seconds, to remember the tune of it, but I couldn't.

"I am so mad at him, Sasha." I could tell she was crying. I heard it in her voice.

"Don't," I said. "Don't cry, or you'll make me cry. I've already been messed up enough today."

"I thought you were going to be my sister-in-law," she said.

"Don't do that, Bailey."

"I'm sorry. I'm so sorry I know that's selfish of me to say, but I can't take it. Are you sure it has to be over? I was afraid of this. Are you sure he did it? I'm so mad at him. I don't believe it."

"What do you mean you were afraid of it?" I asked, instantly overanalyzing her comment.

"I just feared this would happen," she said. "That y'all would break up someday. Are you okay? What happened? When was it?"

"Yesterday."

"Valentine's Day?"

"Yes. I was supposed to be at rehearsal for West Side Story, but we got out early, and I went to his apartment. He was with somebody else."

She was silent.

All I heard was silence and then a sigh.

When she finally spoke she said, "I'm so sorry, Sasha. I don't know what to say."

"You don't have to say anything, I was just texting to let you know because it, you know, changes things. I won't be going to your aunt's for Easter."

"What will you do?"

"For Easter? I don't know."

"No, in general. I want to make sure you're okay."

"Yeah, right now I'm working. I'm about to close the store."

"You're working at Kramer's right now? Or tutoring?"

"No, I'm at Kramer's. A guy just came in here and bought me a thirty-dollar box of chocolate."

"What? Who? Nick?"

"No. I don't know who it was. His name was Warren. He came in to shop. He bought two boxes and left one of them here."

I left out a lot of details of that story simply because I did not feel like retelling it at the moment.

"Was he trying to flirt with you?"

"No, he was just being nice. He bought himself more than he gave me. He didn't care what I put in the box. That one transaction was more than half of the register total of my whole shift."

Still, I didn't mention that he noticed me crying. I didn't want her to feel bad about that. I didn't want her to imagine me working with my swollen face hidden behind a pair of dark sunglasses.

"That's a cool thing to happen," she said. "That was nice of him. Don't you get to eat as much chocolate as you want, anyway?"

"Not really. I could take a piece if I wanted, but not a whole box like this. I'll take it home and share it with my roommates."

"Does August know about you and Nick?" she asked.

I had always been close to my brother, so she assumed the answer would be 'yes'.

"No," I said. "I haven't told anyone. It happened last night, and I basically just came out of my room to go to work. I've only answered a couple of texts today, and I was vague. I thought Nick might've told you. I was wondering why you didn't text me."

"No, he didn't," she said. "Did you fight, you and him?"

"No. I just told him I saw him cheating, and that was that. I said it was over, and I haven't talked to him since. I haven't talked to anyone else about it, either. Not even August."

"You can't do that, Sasha, that's not healthy for you."

"I'm fine," I said. "I'm getting into a band called The Clash. I'm thinking about saving up to get a moped, a Vespa."

"Are you okay?" she said.

"Yes," I said, laughing a little. "It's not that weird of me to say I want a Vespa."

"I know that," she said. "I'm just so mad right now. I wish I was there. I wish there was something I could do. Can I call Nick? Is there anything that can be done between you two?"

"No. I don't think there is. I'm sad. Believe me, I'm sad. It changes a lot in my life. But I don't think I could go back to feeling the way I felt about him, not after hearing him lie to me so easily. William, too. It hurt that he knew about it and lied to me. I'm sorry, Bailey. I know they're your brothers."

"I know they are, but I'm so sorry this happened, Sasha. I can't believe it. I don't know why he would've done it. You're amazing, I hope you know that. He really screwed up."

I did not feel that way at the moment, but I lied and said that I did.

I talked to Bailey for a few more minutes before letting her go so that I could close the store.

Chapter 5

Four months later
June
Ryan and Bailey's wedding

I was in a fragile state, and I had been that way all day. I had gotten over Nick, but I hadn't seen him at all since we broke up, and tonight that would change.

Bailey had just graduated and moved back home, and now she and her boyfriend, Ryan, were tying the knot. I had seen Bailey since she moved home, and we had talked about everything that happened between her brother and me. I hadn't made peace with Nick, though. I didn't plan to do so, I just hoped I could avoid him at the wedding.

Bailey was marrying into Memphis royalty. The Fairchild family owned an iconic theater in Memphis called the Blackbird, and after tonight, Bailey would live in the same building as the theater, upstairs in a gorgeous apartment with rooftop access.

The wedding ceremony and reception would all take place downstairs, in the main theater, which was breathtaking—a gem in our city. As far as I knew, there had never been a wedding there, though.

I went to the ceremony with my brother, August, and a few of our other friends who were actors with the Memphis Players. It felt good to show up in a pack. I had also been on a diet for a few weeks leading up to the ceremony, and I felt confident in my dress.

They held the ceremony on stage, which was cool and like a scene from a play. We were all sitting in the audience—everyone except for Bailey, Ryan, and the guy who officiated it. They didn't have bridesmaids and groomsmen. It was different and simple, and the set pieces they chose for the stage made it look like a rustic, old church house. It was a fairy tale wedding for a stage actress.

Bailey had played a bride before and had a much larger stage wedding than this one. This was a simple and understated version of something Bailey loved so much. We all yelled and clapped when they kissed, and then dozens of staff came running in, and the stage changed. A band quickly set up, and before we knew it, the stage had been transformed into a party area with a band and a dance floor.

People set up backstage with food and drinks, and the stage and aisles filled up with guests who began mingling.

Nick was there, but everything was so fast and busy that I wasn't forced to look at him. I surrounded myself with my friends, in a shield like those buffalo who form a circle around the baby to keep it safe. I had an awareness of Nick's general whereabouts, and I simply avoided looking in his direction.

I knew he looked good, and I knew he was there alone. Those things had been relayed to me by other people. I couldn't, however, bear to speak to him or even stare directly at him. I was happy for Bailey, though, and I smiled and acted normal the whole time, talking to my friends and doing my best to seem unaffected.

I danced a few songs and smiled like I hardly even noticed that Nick existed. It was difficult, though. I was happy for my friend, but I struggled with feelings of guilt about being preoccupied with Nick's whereabouts all night instead of enjoying the reception. It had been exhausting, honestly. I was feeling hyper-self-conscious at a moment when I was trying to be selfless, and it was tiring.

At the moment, I was standing near one of the tables that was set up on the right side of the stage. August was there with me, and so was Gina. We had just come off the dancefloor because it was a slow song, and none of us had a dance partner at the moment.

Tori came over to us with her sights set on August. She looked like she was up to something. "August, would you dance with me? I love this song so much, and I don't have a partner."

"What is this song?" I asked.

"You don't know it? It's called *Better With You*," Tori said. "It's by Warren Manning. My man."

"I like him, too," Gina said.

"You guys like country music?" I asked, making a face and listening to the song. It was country, but it was soulful… the kind of country music I could tolerate. Plus, I liked the guy's voice. "I could see how you like this one, I guess. I usually don't like country, but this is okay."

"I know, but this guy's amazing," Tori said. "Come dance with me, pleeease." She pulled August along, and he went onto the dancefloor with her, leaving me standing there with Gina.

"I've never heard this song," I said, finding it odd that I liked the sound of it.

"It's that guy Tori and Anne-Marie went to see in St. Louis."

"Oh, really? I thought that was some rock concert."

"No, it was this guy, Warren Manning," Gina said. "This song was on the soundtrack of Gone Before Midnight. Tori loves him. He's the one on her phone screen—that guy with the Cubs baseball cap."

I just shrugged because I wasn't familiar with Tori's lock screen. I was too busy making sure Nick was still a safe distance from me.

"What's up pea-pole?" Shep said, coming over and high-fiving us like it was the first time he'd seen us all night. Malcolm Shepherd, or Shep to all of us. He was one of the ring leaders at Memphis Players—the loud, funny, life-of-the-party type. Everyone loved Shep. He had been busy with the date he brought to the wedding tonight—a new girl named Kyla.

"Where's your lady?" I asked.

"She went to the restroom," Shep said. He winked. "And she's not quite my lady yet. It's only the second date. That's why we're skipping the slow songs… I'm not trying to let her fall in love with me yet." He reached for Gina's drink, which looked like some kind of punch. "Can I have a sip of this? What were you guys talking about?"

"This song," Gina said, handing her drink to Shep. "Sasha's never heard of it."

"Oh, Warren Manning, *cause baby, I'm better with you*," Shep sang, unrepentantly even though a completely different part of the song was playing. He did it loudly and with a southern drawl. Boy, was Shep a showman.

"I'm getting out my phone to show Sasha a picture," Gina said, digging in her clutch.

"Of what?" I asked, feeling distracted by the thought of Nick moving around in the room. I was thinking about him and his whereabouts when Gina shoved a phone in front of my face.

I blinked at the images that popped up on the screen.

"I know that guy," I said, gawking at the phone in disbelief. I reached for Gina's arm, pulling her closer.

"I knew you'd know him," she said. "He's not like the regular country guys… he's bluesy. He loves

Elvis. I read an article about him one time when I was sitting in the dentist's office, waiting to get a cavity filled. It was in People. He grew up in Nashville, but he's different."

"I don't know him from music," I said, still staring at the screen in disbelief. "I've never heard his music. I meant that I *really* know him. I met him in real life. He came into Kramer's."

"Warren Manning went into *Kramer's Chocolates*?" Gina asked, blinking at me with wide eyes, staring. "Are you sure it was him?"

"Yes. He introduced himself as Warren. He had a big, black truck that looked like the secret service."

"Warren Manning bought chocolate candy from Sasha," Shep said in an amused tone.

I thought of the interaction with him that night.

It was the day after Valentine's Day—the day after Nick. Warren had swooped in to save me then, and he was somehow doing it again now, just when I was worried about Nick again. I smiled a genuine smile as I handed Gina her phone.

"He bought chocolate from me, and he bought chocolate *for* me."

I proceeded to tell them the story of the night I met Warren Manning. I left out the details about me crying. I downplayed the heartbreak and ramped up the other details of meeting him. I was insecure and uncertain of myself at the wedding, and it felt so good to have a funny, interesting story to tell. Everyone loved it. Shep repeated it to his lady friend when she walked up, and then they all repeated it to Tori when she and August joined the group.

"I would have absolutely died," Tori said. "I can't believe you had the chance to go in his truck and stick your hand under his seat, and all you did was give him a pencil. You were going to be able to touch his phone, Sasha! What came over you? Why did you give him that freaking pencil?"

I laughed at her for being so serious about it.

"How close were you? Physically, how close were you to him?"

"I don't know, we walked by each other, and I stood next to him. I'm pretty sure I touched his hand."

Tori yelped and swooned, and I laughed. I remembered him being a lady-killer, but I had been so focused on other things that night, that I didn't give much thought to meeting that stranger. All I knew was that his kindness was one of the things that gave me strength during the breakup.

It was amazing that this Warren guy was here to help me again. My story about meeting him was a hit at the wedding, and it made me confident and happy at a time when I was struggling.

Maybe it was the change in my countenance that made Nick come over to me. I was still standing there talking to Gina, and a few others when he walked up to us. I turned and saw him when he tapped me on the shoulder.

My smile fell.

"Sorry," he said, taking a step back.

"It's okay. I just didn't know you were standing there."

Nick looked around. "Cool wedding, huh?"

"Yeah, yeah, it is. It's neat. I loved it. And I'm happy for your sister."

"I know. Me too. I love Ryan."

"Yeah," I said. I stayed silent after that, and we both gave each other awkward glances and smiles.

"You look good," he said.

But at the same exact time, I said, "The crab is amazing."

It was the only thing I had taken a bite of so far at the wedding, so it seemed like a logical topic.

He nodded to my statement, and I ignored his. "I ate some of those crab things," Nick said. "All of the food is good. Ryan's friend cooked it, and he's a famous chef."

Nick and I already had conversations about Zack Horner. He knew I knew who Zack was, but I just smiled and went along with it. "Yeah, it's delicious," I said.

"Hey, Sasha, I wanted to take you to meet someone." I felt my brother's hand on my arm, and I looked at him. He glanced at Nick. "Hey, Nick, I'm going to borrow my sister," August said. "I'm really happy for your sister. Beautiful wedding."

August was quick and no-nonsense. He gave Nick a quick smile and pulled me away from the conversation. We walked toward the edge of the stage and went down the steps.

August was my hero in that moment.

I truly hadn't seen Nick coming and I had not been expecting him to come up to me.

"I'm sorry, but no," August said.

"What do you mean?" I asked, smiling at his back as we walked.

He turned and looked at me. "I saw the way he was looking at you," he said.

"Like what?" I asked.

"Like he was about to try to get back together with you."

I let out a laugh. "That wouldn't work, anyway."

Chapter 6

Three months later
September

I was officially a senior, and this year was off to such a better start than the last one. I was keeping up with my work, my bills, and my studies. I was not currently taking part in a musical production, so that made things easier. The Memphis Players were about to audition for the winter show, but I was sitting this one out so that I could focus on school and concentrate on improving my GPA from the dip it took last year. I had no plans, at this point, to go to graduate school, but I also had no job prospects yet, so I wanted to keep my options open.

Either way, I was already on the road to success this semester. I had introduced myself to all of my professors, and I was organized and ready to respond to all the information they presented us. I had already taken some notes and quizzes, and so far, so good.

I went to work at the chocolate shop one Tuesday afternoon in mid-September, and there was a package waiting for me. It was addressed with a return label from RCA Records in Nashville, and it was roughly the same size as a brick, though not as heavy.

"What's this?" I asked, seeing it on the desk when I went in the back room to clock in.

Sharon stared down at the package in question. "Oh, that came yesterday. You were supposed to sign for it, and Dianna forged your signature because she didn't know when you were working again. It was addressed to Sasha Bee, so she wasn't even sure if it was yours. She was worried sick about signing for it. I'm surprised she didn't tell you about it."

"No, I had no idea it was here," I said. "I haven't talked to Dianna."

"Is your name Sasha Bee?"

"Not really. I mean, the Sasha part's right."

"I don't know what to tell you. It's from RCA Records, so I thought it was like one of those deals from Columbia House. Do you remember those? You're too young for that, but I used to order CDs from a place where you'd get a bunch free. It was some kind of deal where you get ten of them for a quarter if you pay shipping."

"I didn't order any free CDs," I said, turning over the package.

"Do you know that thing I'm talking about?" Sharon asked nostalgically. "That service?"

"No. I'm just trying to imagine what this is."

"It doesn't look the same size as CDs anyway," Sharon said. "And that place was called Columbia House, not RCA. It might be a scam, though," she added. "I'd be careful if I were you—especially if it's a bunch of free music."

I smiled at her. She had been on her way out, and I hesitated, not opening the package until she walked out of the room. Someone had just clocked out, so Sharon and I were the only two there. I opened the package. It was taped up like it had been packed by a human and not some machine. I unwrapped the outer paper and realized that there was a small recycled box inside—something that had already been mailed one time before. I opened that box, and peered inside to find a significant stack of cash.

Cash?

In disbelief, I used my thumb to pick up the corner of the stack. I thumbed through it and realized there was quite a lot of money there. They were hundred-dollar bills, and they were so new that it looked like monopoly money. Quickly, I closed the flaps of that box, looking around and wondering if there were cameras in this room. I knew there were. *Who would send me a box full of cash, and who would mail it to my part-time job instead of my apartment?* I figured the money was possibly fake. Either way, it was sketchy. I couldn't help but be curious, though, so I stood up and took that box directly to the restroom.

I saw there had been a piece of paper with the stack of money, and I took it somewhere private to inspect it. There was nowhere else to sit in that small bathroom, so I put the toilet seat down and took a seat there. I reached into the box to get the note that was lying on top of the stack of bills. I stared inside curiously. There was a band around the hundred dollar bills. It was gold and it had a dollar amount written on it. The band told me there was ten-thousand dollars wrapped up inside of it, and my initial reaction was to feel scared, like I was being trapped in some way.

There was a round, stainless steel trashcan with a lid nearby, and I set the box down on it, standing and stepping away warily. I stared down at the note, which was still in my hand. It was folded twice, and I unfolded it and read the words. The note was handwritten on a piece of copy paper. The paragraphs were centered and took up the entire page.

Sasha,

My name is Warren Manning. Earlier this year, I came into the chocolate shop where you worked. You were dancing to The Clash and wearing Converse, and we talked for a while. My phone was stuck, remember?

Anyway, I wrote a song about our encounter that night. It's called Someone Else's Valentine, and it features a girl like you who was doing the same things you were doing that night when we met. I changed some of it for songwriting purposes, but she's got on two different shoes and she's dancing like you were.

I've been informed by lawyers that I owe you no compensation for the inspiration. I have been strictly prohibited to write this note to you or send money at all. That is why there's cash enclosed instead of a check.

I, however, on a personal level, wanted to reach out and let you know that the song exists and that you were the inspiration behind it. I loved meeting you that night. You didn't seem to know my work, so I thought there was a chance you'd never hear the song. I've thought about you since we met. I hope you're doing well and that there's no more wearing sunglasses at night.

The song will release next month on an EP, but I'll email it to you early. I would be counting on you for secrecy since it hasn't been released yet. I feel like I can trust you. You can call or email me. I would love to hear from you.

Much love, and thanks for the inspiration,

Warren Manning

He included his phone number and email address.

I started at the top, and read the note again. I was in the bathroom for at least five minutes, reading the note and looking at the cash, and feeling unable to believe any of it. I was smiling absentmindedly to myself and thinking when I heard a loud knock on the bathroom door.

"Are you okay?" Sharon asked, causing me to jump and quickly close the note.

"Yeah, I'm coming," I said.

"I was curious about your box."

"Oh, it was just junk mail," I said.

I felt a little bad about the lie, but I had just been charged with keeping all of it a secret. I did not have my bag with me, so I stashed the note in my back pocket and the stack of bills in my shirt. I carried the empty box out with me. Sharon was in the front retail space by that point and she saw me walk out of thc bathroom.

"No music?" she asked.

"No music," I said, telling the truth.

I went to the office and discreetly placed the cash into my purse, burying it under several things so it was nowhere near the top. I also buried my purse in the office.

I had a hard time processing everything. The package, the money, and the note—it was all on my mind constantly that night. I didn't mention it to Sharon, and I didn't mention it to Mitchell when he clocked in to help me close.

And then when I left, I didn't call August, Gina, or anyone else. I didn't call my parents. I kept the note and the money to myself.

I went to school the following day, and I saw some of my other friends there, but still, I didn't tell a soul. I stopped at a coffee shop on my way home from school and I broke one of those hundred dollar bills.

I received ninety-four dollars in change, and I put it in my wallet. Somehow, the money felt totally different now that I knew it actually spent like regular bills. No one had stopped me, and no alarms had gone off.

I was still in disbelief as I drove home from that coffee shop. I found Warren's music, and put on his most recent album. Someone Else's Valentine wasn't on it, but I knew it wouldn't be since it hadn't been released yet. I stared at his profile picture and felt nervous and excited that this was the same person who had written me a long note.

I listened to his music all the way home, and during that time, I fell in love with his voice and the sound of his music. I could see how Tori had a gigantic crush on him. I was now jealous of this crush. I felt hot blood rush to my face when I thought about Tori and how much she loved Warren.

I had his phone number and I wanted to use it, and now I had to worry about Tori getting her feelings hurt or feeling jealous. I couldn't worry about that. I didn't let myself worry. I turned up the music and enjoyed my coffee and the nine-thousand-nine-hundred-ninety-something dollars I had left over from it.

It was later that night when I finally composed a text to send to the number on the note. By that time,

I had some time to think about it, and I had listened to all of the albums that he had released.

Me:

It's Sasha Faulkner from Memphis. I got your package and I wanted to thank you! You didn't have to do that. How cool about the song. Thank you so much! And yes, I'm all better, no more sunglasses.

I pressed send without giving it too much thought.

It was only minutes later when I heard back from him.

Warren:

I was wondering if you were going to text.

I grinned as I stared down at the screen. I was sitting in my own bedroom with no one around. I was normally the type to confide in my friends and family, and it was odd and out of character for me to keep this whole thing a complete secret. Maybe it was Tori's feelings for him that made me do it, or maybe I just couldn't believe it was real.

Me:

I did. And I'd love to hear the song, but I can wait until it comes out if that's better for you.

Warren:

It is better for me, but I'm still willing to send it to you. I trust you not to share. Send me your email.

I grinned the whole time I typed. I texted him with my email address, and within minutes I heard from him. He had attached the song along with an email that was lengthier than any of our texts.

Hey Sasha,

This song is going to be the second to last title on the EP. This is the demo. The regular version has already been recorded, but this is all I have to send. You'll recognize the character in the song as yourself. I was inspired by meeting you that night. I knew it would turn into a song. I started it on my way home. I'm happy with how it came out, and I hope you're happy with it, too.

Warren

Chapter 7

The song itself was a digital file of some sort, and I was able to play it directly from my email. I started the song, and it began playing through the speaker in my phone. I heard an intro with an acoustic guitar, and then he began to sing…

I saw the way he broke her heart,
refused to be her Valentine.
He made her cry.
How he missed the mark.

But, oh, she put on her dancing shoes,
One that was pink and one that was blue,
And she danced, oh, I saw her dance,
and her heart hurt no more.

I thought she was broken,
I saw he left her crying.
But come next year, it's him who'll hurt,
Cause she'll be someone else's Valentine.

But, oh, she put on her dancing shoes,
One that was pink and one that was blue,
And she danced, oh, I saw her dance,
and her heart hurt no more.

And then I'll wait for the right time,
to go to her and say,
I liked your shoes,
I liked your smile.
I'll pick up that guy's slack.

Now she's someone else's Valentine,
and I knew that someone would be mine

And, oh, she put on her dancing shoes,
I don't even care what color they are,
And she dances, oh, I watch her dance,
and her heart hurts no more.

I felt a knot in my throat during the whole song, but it grew during the last half. I was on the verge of tears. His voice was like a soulful soothing balm. It was easy to get lost in the sound of it and not even hear the lyrics.

But how could I ignore these lyrics?

And what was I to make of them?

I played the song a few times in a row just so that I could listen closely to what he was saying.

My heart absolutely pounded when he sang that I would be his. I knew he had warned me that it was a song and that parts of it weren't true, but oh how I wished it was all true.

It had been twenty minutes since Warren sent that email, and I knew I needed to respond. I didn't know what to say, though. I was starstruck, and I found it difficult to get over my own adrenaline and excitement and think of what to say. I had to respond, but I couldn't assume the song meant he had any feelings for me. I had to be vague.

I typed an email back to him.

Warren,

What a great song! I loved it. I didn't realize you were such a talented musician when we met. I heard your music later. I know you said this wasn't the final recording, but I loved it and wouldn't change a thing. You sound so good. Thank you so much for including me in your lyrics and for sharing. You were right to trust me. I won't tell a soul, I promise. Also, thank you for sending money. It was unnecessary, and I still have all but six dollars of it if you need it back. I'm happy just to be featured in a song.

All the best,

Sasha

I pressed send.

I didn't think twice about anything I said. The weirdest part about it was that I wasn't going to tell a soul about Warren or the song. I knew that I would hold it inside. That was actually unbelievable. August was my number one confidant. It had been that way since we were babies. I told him everything. But this latest development with

Warren—this felt too big and insane to tell even my brother.

Communicating with a famous person was not something I had ever pictured myself doing. I had never been the type to have celebrity crushes.

I didn't necessarily expect to hear back from Warren after I emailed, but at the same time, I hoped I would. I started to feel crush-like feelings.

It was fifteen minutes later when I got a text.

It was from Warren. It was short, but the words caused me to get all wound up inside.

Warren:
Is that all you have to say about the song?

My body started buzzing the instant I read the text.

Me:
Did you get my email?

He texted me back right away.

Warren:
Yes, and it was vague.

I blinked at my phone. He seemed so confident and comfortable, even in his texts. I had to be vague. I wasn't just going to come out and say that he was the most gorgeous guy I had ever seen and that I was now all worked up because of his talent. I felt like Tori. I couldn't believe I had a crush on a country singer. It didn't seem real.

None of this seemed real.

I sat on the edge of my bed, feeling like I could hardly believe what was happening to me. It took me a minute to think of a response and compose a text. I didn't want to be too forward, and I also didn't want to leave him hanging. I tried several different responses before I settled on one.

Me:

I really loved the song! I assume the shoes and the dancing were really the only part that applied to me.

It took him thirty minutes to text me back, and in that time, I doubted and second-guessed myself a thousand times.

Warren:
I'm in Chicago right now.

Me:
I'm in Memphis.

Warren:
Where in Memphis?

Me:

My apartment.

Warren:
No work?

Me:
No work today. Full day of school.

Warren:
Senior year?

Me:
Yes! Yay.

Warren:
How's accounting going?

Me:
Great. I'm acing this semester.

Warren:
Can I call you?

I swallowed past the lump in my throat. My hands shook as I typed a response.

Me:
Yes. Now?

Warren:

Yes.

I read his text and I sat there staring at my phone, wondering if I should expect it to ring any second.

My phone rang, and his number showed up on my screen. It wasn't even his name. I hadn't created a contact—this was all too unbelievable.

I was in a dreamlike state when I answered the phone.

"Hello," I said.

"Hey, Sasha?"

"Yeah."

"Did you mcan to write that you were acting in a play this semester?"

"No, I'm not doing the play right now. Sometimes I sit one out."

"So, you meant to say that you were acing the semester?" he asked. "Getting good grades?"

"Yes. I'm overachieving this year to get my GPA back up."

"What's your last name?"

"Faulkner."

"Sasha Faulkner?"

"Yep."

"I just wrote Sasha Bee on that package."

"I know. I'm glad it got to me. What was that name?"

"Middle?"

"Middle?" I asked.

"I was hoping it would pass as a middle name and get delivered to you. What's your middle name?"

"Leigh."

"Sasha Leigh Faulkner," he said. "I was almost right with Bee."

"Why'd you say Bee?"

"You're like a bumblebee. A honeybee."

I could hear the smile in his voice, and my heart ached. "What are you doing in Chicago? I mean, you don't have to tell me, but—"

"I'm here for fun," he said. "I have a friend who plays football here. I met him back in Nashville when he played for the Titans."

"Oh, that kind of football," I said. "NFL?"

"Yes. Jamie Bowen."

"Oh, my gosh, you're friends with Jamie Bowen? Wide receiver?"

"Yeah, he's my boy. I'm sitting next to his pool right now."

My heart skipped a beat at the picture that flashed across my mind. I was talking to a famous singer who was currently sitting in Jamie Bowen's backyard. The likelihood of any of this was so non-existent that nerves weren't even a factor. I just talked to him like I would talk to anyone else. I was naturally myself. That was all I could do. If I started to try to be cool in front of him, I knew I would fail, so I defaulted to being myself. I told him that I loved football and was a fan of Jamie's.

We talked about his trip and the game he saw the day before. He told me details about it… that he couldn't ever do anything embarrassing because he had to be ready at any moment to see his own face on the jumbotron.

He asked about my studies and my life in regard to friends and work. He seemed interested in small facts about me—asking me what I liked to do as a kid, and what my parents were like.

I asked him some of the same questions.

He had a much harder childhood than me. He had grown up with a single mom who was chasing her own dream of being a singer. She also drank quite a bit. She was still living in Nashville, but alcohol had been an ongoing problem. Warren took care of her, but there was an underlying strained tone to their relationship because she had some bitterness about her own disappointments.

Warren openly admitted that his own hardships in life were the very thing that made him able to write and perform in a way that audiences connect with. He gave credit to his crappy childhood for making him famous.

I had looked into him a little bit during the last couple of days, and I read some of the same things he was saying, but Warren shared details and feelings that made it all feel more personal.

We talked for an hour, and he was humble and real, and one hundred percent human. I easily tuned out the fact that he was famous. I forgot that I should be intimidated by him.

I was lying on my bed, staring at the ceiling when he said, "Hey, I have to let you go, Jamie's here and we're going to get something to eat."

"Yeah, oh, yeah, of course. Okay, great talking to you. Thanks for everything, Warren."

"Can I call you again?" he asked.

"Sure," I said, trying not to sound surprised.

"Tomorrow?"

"Yeah, definitely. I have to write a paper in the morning, but I could take a call. I work in the afternoon, but I'll have breaks, and… anyway, yes."

"I'll just text you in the morning," he said.

"Sounds good," I said, going back to those feelings of nervousness now that he was asking about talking to me again.

"Okay," he said.

"Okay," I added, smiling.

"I'm glad you texted me, Sasha."

"I'm glad, too," I said.

"I'll talk to you tomorrow, then."

"Okay," I agreed.

"Sasha?"

"Yeah?"

"Is it weird of me to ask for a picture?"

I thought he said *the* picture, and I said, "What picture?"

"Of you."

"Of me?"

"One of your face," he said. "I guess I can try to look you up online, but I'd rather you just text me a picture."

"I will," I agreed. "I'm taking one now, and I'll send it."

"Thank you," he said.

We said 'goodbye' and hung up the phone, and I took a picture of myself right that very second. I sat up on my bed, getting a good view of my room behind me.

I took a real picture. I wasn't trying to look bad, but I wasn't trying to look good, either. On a scale of one to ten with how good of a photo I could possibly take of myself, this one was an even six.

I smiled directly into the lens and took a few quick photos in a row. I chose the best of the three, not overthinking it. I had makeup on from earlier, but it wasn't a whole lot, and I felt no need to try to be something I wasn't. Honestly, part of me probably wanted to turn him off in that moment. If Warren was the type who would lose interest after seeing the real me, it's better that he does it now.

I was about to send a heart emoji to accompany the photo, but I changed my mind. I only sent the photo—the semi-flattering photo.

I was still staring at the text screen when I saw a text come in. He sent me a picture of himself that was natural and real, just like mine.

I sent him a heart emoji.

He sent me a heart emoji back.

I put my phone on my bed, knowing our communication was over for now. My heart still raced. My nerves had gotten steady during the time when our conversation was flowing on the phone, but the photos and the fact that we made plans to talk again made me feel all worked up.

It was the real Warren Manning in the photograph—the blue-eyed, baby-faced troublemaker. This guy had it all. He was country music's bad boy with a nostalgic, soulful voice. He had a roughness to his voice that was a bit surprising coming from someone with such a perfect face. Warren didn't have his hat on, and his dark brown long-ish wavy hair fell over his forehead. He hadn't tried too hard, and at the same time, the photo was perfect. He was unbelievably handsome. I knew as much from searching him on the internet, but receiving a current selfie from his exact location was fun and put the biggest smile on my face.

Chapter 8

My eyes opened at 5:30am the following morning.

I was usually an 8:30 girl, but I was amped up from talking to Warren. I tried to go back to sleep, but it was no use. I got out of bed with plans to get to work on my school paper. I was out of coffee, though. My roommate had some, but I had already used hers once recently.

I planned to do some of my paper at a coffee shop, anyway, so I figured I would get dressed and go early. I made a note to go by the grocery store on the way home so that I had coffee for tomorrow. I put on some leggings and a sweatshirt and pulled my hair into a ponytail.

I was at the coffee shop, sitting in a corner, by 6:15. For a short while, I was the only person there. People came in and out, but I was the only one who settled at a table for any length of time. After seven, it filled up, and there were people sitting all around me at tables and booths.

I had my headphones in the whole time, always with white noise playing. I liked having coffee shop smells and sites around me and didn't find it distracting at all. I was easily able to focus on my work and get a lot done while I sat there. I worked for a couple of hours, and then I took a break. I did two sudoku puzzles and some people-watching for ten minutes while I ate the rest of the fruit cup from earlier.

I worked for another forty-five minutes after that. I was still sitting there, typing on my laptop when I got a call.

It was Warren, and a rush of excitement hit me when I saw his name (which was saved on my phone now).

I answered. "Hello?" I said speaking at just the right volume for him to hear me without drawing attention.

"Hey, are you busy?"

I grinned at the sound of his voice. "I'm at a coffee shop, but I was about to leave," I said. I began packing up my things as I used my shoulder to hold the phone to my ear. It only took a second. All I had was my laptop and a handful of trash.

"I don't mean to make you stop what you're doing."

"It's okay. I've been here a long time already. I've gotten a lot done. Hang on one second." I stood from the table. "Okay," I said, a second later when I was on my way out. I tossed the trash intó the bin by the door. "I was working on a paper, but I got way more done on it than I expected to. I'm in the middle of walking out right… in one second, I'll be… okay, I'm outside now," I said once I stepped onto the sidewalk.

"You're writing at a coffee shop?" he asked.

"Yeah, I like doing that," I said. "I like to have something to look at, some action happening around me. And I have no problem being productive. I got a lot done—almost that whole paper. What are you doing?" I asked.

"I got up and worked out. Just now, I had to meet with a woman, Becky, who works as my assistant. She told me about some scheduling things, which I didn't take in. She'll have to tell me again—send me notes. I'm waiting for Jamie right now. He's still at the training facility, but gets off at noon today."

I tried not to think about the female assistant. I blew past that bit of information.

"All I have to do today is go to the grocery store and then work a shift from two to six at the chocolate shop."

"What do you need from the grocery store?"

"Some coffee and a few other things—oatmeal, frozen chicken nuggets, and brownie mix. Just the essentials."

He laughed. "We've both been busy. I'm already tired," he said. "Jamie worked out early this morning, so I got up and went to the training facility with him. I hung out with the team."

"Oh, yeah? Have you done that before?"

"Yeah, I've been over there. Football players usually like my music, so I get a warm welcome. I'm sure not all of them like it, but they pretend they do. They always ask me to sing a song or two, and then I get to sit in on the team meeting and hear a few notes from their coach."

"That's amazing. I've seen that kind of thing on TV, but I can't imagine being there."

"It's a cool environment—locker room camaraderie is fun."

"It's wonderful to have a friend who plays pro football."

"I know, and I love Jamie. He's a good human. I wouldn't come all the way out here just to get a tour of the Bears' locker room. I could do that kind of thing in Nashville. Jamie's my boy."

"Did you say it was this morning that you went there?"

"Yes."

"You've had a busy day already."

"I know. It was fun, though."

"Are you back at Jamie's?"

"Yeah, but he's still at work. I drove separate."

"What are you doing?"

"I'm… at a swimming pool, surrounded by a bunch of women."

"Are you really?" I asked, smiling.

"No, and I don't know why I said that just now. I'm trying to get a rise out of you."

I laughed.

"But you don't care."

I laughed again. "I'm sure you find yourself surrounded by women all the time," I said. "I can't start caring about that."

"Why not? Maybe you should be jealous."

"Stop."

"Stop what?"

"You're being weird."

"No, I'm not," he said.

"Have you ever been to the Biltmore Estate?"

"In Carolina?" he asked.

"Yes. North Carolina. Asheville. Have you ever been there?" I asked.

"No. What's that have to do with you being jealous?"

I let out a humorless laugh. "Warren, don't mess with me."

"I'm not."

"I just want to talk about something else," I said, feeling flustered, and knowing in my heart that there was no possibility of longevity in a relationship. "That's why I was talking about the Biltmore. It's amazing. It's the largest private home in the US. How big is your house?"

"Not even close to record-setting big. I have two houses, and both of them put together are still way smaller than that."

"You have two houses?"

"Yes. One that's close to Nashville, and another that's out in the woods, forty miles on the other side of Knoxville. I have a little property at my Nashville house, too, but, there's better fishing and wildlife out there at my East Tennessee place. And nobody really knows or cares that I'm out there. I go out there to be alone. It's peaceful. I'll have to show you sometime."

"Why are you telling me all these things?" I asked.

"Because I like you," he said. "I'm trying to, but you're not letting me."

"Maybe you only want to because you think I'm not letting you."

"What's that supposed to mean?"

"I don't know. You're you and I'm me, and the likely outcome, in this scenario, is that my heart gets broken."

"Your heart? I'm the one who's been liking you since we met. I'm the one who wrote a song. When have you ever written me a song?"

He was being playful, and I grinned and bit my lip even though he couldn't see me, or maybe because he couldn’t see me. I opened my mouth to speak, but I felt choked and couldn't think of what to say. I cleared my throat.

"Warren, this kind of thing feels unreal."

"It feels unreal to me too. I go to Memphis for one thing, and that's Elvis. I try to go on his birthday, but this year I was late. I went in February instead, and you know how it went… I drove off that night, and you stayed in my mind."

"I was a mess."

"That wasn't what I saw."

He was being serious, and I felt overwhelmed. I wanted to believe all this was true, but I couldn't. I knew he wasn't going to tell his family about me or make any sort of commitment to me. Writing about me in a song was one thing, but it's something entirely different to actually commit to dating someone. I had already hashed out these feelings since we had been back in touch, and I reminded myself of them during the pause in our conversation. It was insane, though, that he was saying such sweet things, and it was easy to get swept away.

"Why are you being quiet?"

"I don't know what to say. This whole thing feels like a dream. I have people in my life that I'm close to, and I usually tell them things. And this whole thing with you, I haven't told a soul about it. I don’t mind, but that's just another thing that makes it seems unreal. I like you and everything, but I'm trying to be real."

"Ouch."

"What? Why ouch?" I asked.

"Because, I'm telling you that I like you and you're just like, 'let's keep it real'."

"Well, seriously, Warren. I have to. I’m not just going to let myself be a sitting duck who lets a rockstar break my heart just because he wrote a song about my Converse."

"Why are you being so mean?"

The question made me feel bad.

"I'm not trying to be mean… and I'm sorry if I'm coming across that way. It's a great song. I'm probably being mean for the same reason that I sent you a bad picture last night."

"It's not a bad picture, but why?"

"So that you'll leave me alone sooner than later."

There was a silence that was seconds long but seemed like hours. "Do you want me to leave you alone?" he asked.

He was serious. I could hear it in his voice.

"No, I don't want you to," I said, meekly.

I had just pulled up at my apartment. I needed to go grocery shopping, but I figured I would do it later once I was finished with my conversation with Warren. I lived in a small apartment complex, and no one was around. I was overheated from our conversation, and it was cool out, so I turned my car off and sat there in the parking lot with my door open to let in the fresh air.

"I want to get to know you, Sasha. I like you. I want to see you again." His words caused me to experience a warm, flowing feeling in my core.

"I would like to see you again, too," I said. I knew he was going to break my heart eventually, but there was nothing I could do to make myself deny him.

"I get back to Nashville tomorrow at noon. I have to leave town again the following day, but I could meet you halfway sometime tomorrow afternoon. It's three hours, so that's not far, if we meet in the middle."

"Okay," I said, not caring what else I had scheduled.

"I could leave my house sometime around three o'clock. That puts me mid-way at four thirty, and we can hang out for an hour or so before I need to get back."

"Where should we meet?" I asked.

"I don't know. At a park, maybe. A restaurant? We can just sit in my truck, if it comes to that."

"Okay," I said.

"Okay? We're meeting?"

"Yeah, definitely."

"Tomorrow?" he asked.

"Yes. That sounds fun."

"Good! Well, I'm leaving it up to you. Look at a map and choose a place that's halfway. Send me the location, and I'll meet you there at four-thirty."

"All right. Do you want me to text you with an address?"

"Yes, but I'm not trying to get off of the phone with you right now. Jamie's not here, and I'm just standing here, cooking, with you on speakerphone."

"Cooking what?"

"Grilled cheese. He has all kinds of stuff in his fridge, but I was hungry for this. I know you love to cook," he added. "You're probably disappointed that's what I'm making for breakfast."

"No, I love grilled cheese, and I could get into that for breakfast."

"Did you look at a map yet?"

I smiled. "I'm looking at a map now, actually, and it looks like there's a place halfway. Honestly, it depends on where you are in Nashville. I might need to get closer to you."

"No, if you see a place that looks like it's halfway, that's fine."

"There's a restaurant called Patty's at the exit. I think it looks good if we're hungry, and if not, we can just meet there and go somewhere else."

"Okay, send me the address to that place," he said.

"I will."

"I can't believe we're doing this," he said. "Sasha Honeybee Faulkner. The dancing girl."

I let out a little laugh, feeling thankful for my brother and for all the years of my childhood that he had drug my rear end to rehearsals. I was only comfortable dancing like that because I had years of training for shows. All I was doing in that moment was drawing from bits of choreography I had learned. The moves had been embedded in my muscle memory. Whatever I had done, though, had sparked something within Warren, and now he seemed to be pursuing me. I had no idea how long this would last, but there was nowhere else I would possibly be than along for the ride.

Chapter 9

I talked to Warren for what must've been a total of four hours on the phone that day. We talked while I went to the grocery store. I had his voice in my earphones while I was in the store and going through the self-checkout.

Our conversation was oddly familiar—verging on intimate. We shared things and laughed and made jokes that the other one seemed to get even though we had just come into each other's lives.

I talked to him again, around midnight, for another hour. By the end of our conversation, our voices were soft and sticky. Our words were even sticky. There was tension between us—even over the phone. My heart ached to see Warren and be near him. My gut was alive with warm, electric feelings, and I went to bed replaying some of the things we had said to each other on the phone that day. It was way too late when I fell asleep, but I was smiling.

I had class the following day. I was supposed to be there from eleven to two, but I planned on leaving early so that I could go home and get dressed for my big excursion to see him. I looked terrible when we met, and then I took a mediocre photo. Now it was time for me to do my best—try my hardest.

I left class early so that I could go to my apartment and freshen up. I got mostly dressed before class, and then I went home and finished the job, making sure I was fresh as a daisy for my drive to the middle of nowhere, Tennessee.

I texted Warren again this morning before class. His trip home was on track, and we solidified our plans to meet at 4:30. I left my apartment a half-hour early so that I could be sure to make it there on time. I had on jeans and a sweater. I hoped it looked nice and also like I wasn't trying too hard. I was doubtful of all of my choices. I tried to look natural and effortless even though I put quite a lot of thought into getting ready.

It was cool outside, but I was all wound up about seeing Warren, and I ran the air conditioning in my car to keep myself cool. I had dark hair and features, and the sweater I chose was light purple. It was a color I loved and wore quite a bit. I put on some lavender-tinted lip gloss to compliment the color of my shirt. I hoped Warren would kiss me.

I got to the location twenty minutes early, and I went inside the restaurant to use the restroom and check myself in the mirror. They weren't busy this time of day, and I talked to a lady and told her I was waiting for someone and that we didn't need a seat quite yet.

My phone was in my pocket, and it rang when I was on my way back outside to my car. It was my brother, and I smiled as I put it to my ear.

"Hey," I said.

"Hey, where are you? I just went by your apartment and you weren't there."

"I know. I'm not home. Why?"

"We were supposed to hang out."

"Oh, my gosh, August, is that today?"

"Yes, it's today. We texted yesterday. Where are you? You disappeared off the face of the earth."

"No, I haven't. I'm here."

"Where?" he said. "I thought you were going to help me pick out that stuff for my house. I need two bookshelves and a table."

August had been working all through college, and he had just bought his first house. It was a small place, but it was in a nice neighborhood, and I was really proud of him for saving money and doing that.

"I forgot we talked about shopping," I said regretfully.

"Are you working? Did you pick up a shift? I can meet you at Kramer's when you get off. It might still be early enough."

"I'm not working. I'm hanging out with a friend. I actually drove out to the country… we're going to a restaurant out here in the boonies, up off the interstate."

"Who's that?" he asked.

"Who's what?"

"What friend?"

"None of your business."

August hesitated for a few seconds and then he said, "It's a guy."

"That's irrelevant," I said, walking through the parking lot, from the restaurant to the car. "And I'm sorry for saying none of your business. I know it's your business, but… yes. It's a guy."

"Is it Nick?"

"No, it's not Nick. No way. Why would you say that?"

"Because I know he tried to get back with you."

"That was months ago. I haven't talked to him in weeks."

"So, who are you going to meet?"

"I'm not telling you."

"It better not be someone you met on the internet, Sasha."

I laughed. "The internet? What would make you say that?"

"Because you won't tell me who it is."

"It's a guy I met at work," I said. "We're just having dinner, so I'm not telling you details yet. It may not amount to anything. But he's really cool, though. He's a good guy. He's got a good job and everything. I've talked to him enough that I'm not scared of him. He's not a serial killer."

August breathed a sigh. I knew he was annoyed. He was a guy, and he didn't get emotional about things, but I did normally tell him everything, so I could see how this would be weird for him.

"I'm sorry I forgot we were supposed to hang out today," I added. "I want to help you pick out some things. What's all on your list?"

"Oh, the list is long, but as for what I can afford, a couple of bookshelves, and maybe a table. I need somewhere for my books."

I knew his old apartment had built-ins and that August would need a solution for his collection of biographies and spy novels. August also had a lot of beautiful picture books. He was a book lover and collector who had always worked at a bookstore part-time in spite of whatever else he was doing.

"What about tomorrow afternoon? I don't have work, or tutoring, or anything tomorrow."

"What's his name?"

"Who's name?"

"Sasha." My brother said my name as if to tell me to get real and stop messing around.

"Warren."

"Warren?"

"Yeah, but don't repeat it," I said. "To anyone."

"I wouldn't, but it doesn't matter. I've never even met anyone named Warren."

"I know, but still don't mention it," I said. "Don't tell Mom and Dad or anyone from the Players."

"I won't."

"I'll see you tomorrow," I said. "I'm sorry about today."

"Don't worry about it."

I told my brother farewell just as I was sitting in my car again. I felt bad about forgetting my plans with August, but it completely left my mind.

I thought about Warren. I hadn't talked to him since I had been on the road, so I decided to text him.

Me:

I'm here! I've already been in Patty's, and it looks like good food, but I'm waiting in the car. It's out in the country.

I sat there and stared at my text, reading it twice while holding my finger over the delete key. I erased everything but the first two words.

Me:

I'm here!

I pressed send.

It was not even a minute later when I got a text.

Warren:

I'll be there in ten minutes.

I 'loved' his message, and then I set my phone down. Those moments waiting for him to arrive were the most nerve-racking, longest ten minutes of my life. I checked myself in the mirror and then I got back on my phone, searching the internet for random things like a new sports bra or water bottle. I wasted time for what felt like three hours, and then I finally looked up and saw his truck coming down the street.

It was the same blacked-out truck I had seen in the parking lot of Kramer's that night—a big Chevy with all the extras.

It was Warren.

This was happening.

My chest was tight, and I felt short of breath.

Warren was here.

My car was one of the few vehicles in the parking lot. Everything was wide open, and the sun was low in the sky, so it beamed through my windows, causing me to squint. Warren parked right next to me, and he rolled down his passenger's window so that he could talk to me. His truck was significantly higher than my car.

"Come get in my truck!"

He yelled the words before his truck even came to a complete stop, and I grinned as I turned off my car and started getting out.

Chapter 10

Warren Manning

Ten minutes earlier

Warren hadn't touched the gas pedal in what seemed like fifty miles. He had the cruise control set and the radio turned up. He was beyond excited to see Sasha. He had the masculine urge to take her, claim her, make her say she was his—that she would be his forever. He wanted her in a way that made him want to take everything in their relationship faster. He had a vision in his mind of what Sasha looked like, and he found himself wanting to…

Warren rolled down his window, letting the cool air hit him. He had talked to Sasha a lot, and he loved her mind and her kind spirit. She was funny and she understood sports and masculine humor. He loved her personality, but right then, he was thinking about her in other ways. He wanted to hold her, and he needed to cool off. He had music playing in his truck, and he replayed the memory of how she had danced with that mop. Warren found himself physically aching for Sasha.

It was in that moment that he caught sight of a sign on the interstate.

It was Jesus.

There was a full-length picture of Jesus with his arms outstretched, and the billboard said 'Jesus Saves'. There was a phone number with some information about a church written in smaller letters, but Warren didn't look at any of it long enough to read it.

Jesus Saves. The words hit his heart like an actual arrow had been shot. One second, Warren was impatient and pumped up with testosterone, and the next, his heart was broken with some sort of feeling he didn't understand. He tapped his brake and decreased his speed, pulling to the side of the interstate and turning on his hazards.

Warren spoke out loud, praying, talking to God. "What are you trying to say to me? Is this not the right thing? Am I just chasing a feeling here? Ultimately, I want this. I do want this. But I also want to do what's right. Please tell me something."

It was at that instant that Warren's phone rang. It was his mother, and he answered it.

She sniffled before she even said a word, and Warren knew she was crying.

"Mom?"

"I’m fine, honey. I was just looking through this old box."

"What old box?"

"A box with a bunch of stuff in it from when you were a baby. It's got some of your old report cards and stuff."

"I think I know what you're talking about," he said, feeling relieved that she wasn't in trouble.

"It had a letter in it. You got me crying all these years later." She sniffled. "You always were so sweet. My sweet little boy."

"What letter?"

"I think you wrote it in camp one time. Remember that year when I sent you off with Paul and Shelley's kids to church camp?"

"That happened for like six straight years."

"Well, one of those years, I don't know how old you were, you wrote this big long letter—talking about how much you loved Jesus and how you wanted to ask Him to make you a big star so you can have a good life and make your mom proud." Her voice was high-pitched as she spoke and she sniffled. "Isn't that so sweet? You also wrote about your future wife. Can you believe you were even thinking about that? You said this whole thing about saving yourself and how when the right girl came around, you wanted God to tell you, right to your face that she was the one so that you would know it." A pause. "Isn't that sweet? You were such a little man. You wrote 'Jesus saves' real big across the top."

"That's awesome," Warren said, his heart beating faster.

"Well, I love you, and I just wanted to tell you that your dream came true."

"What dream?"

"You became a big star, and you're making your mama proud." Her speech was a little slurred, but her words made perfect sense, and he was thankful for them.

"Thank you," he said.

"You take good care of me," she added.

"Thank you. I love you. And thanks for calling and telling me that about the letter."

"You're welcome. I love you, son."

"I love you, too."

Warren hung up the phone with his mom. He stared at the ceiling of his truck. He knew these events were linked. It was too amazing to be a coincidence.

"Okay, God, I think you're giving me the okay with Sasha, but I'm still that same kid who wrote that note. Can you tell me, please, if you want me to continue on this road to see Sasha?"

The timing was comically accurate.

Warren barely got the sentence out when he heard a pinging sound. The screen on his dash lit up, and there were three simple words on the screen—a name and a two-word sentence.

Sasha:
I'm here!

Warren did not deserve for God to pick out a lady and make it so obvious that she was the one, but it had happened. He was pumped up thinking about seeing her. He really hoped she could fall in love with him, because he was done for. His heart was set on Sasha, and now everything had lined up.

He was smiling uncontrollably as he typed a text to her. He told her that he would be there in ten minutes even though his GPS said fourteen. He would do his best to reach her in ten.

He got back on the interstate and drove as quickly as possible to the exit with the restaurant.

Warren's heart was beating out of his chest. He knew he wanted Sasha before, and now the feeling was intensified. He had undoubtedly heard from God. He could not get to her quickly enough.

Warren found the restaurant and pulled into the parking lot, heading straight for the small Honda that he knew to be Sasha's. She was parked in the back. His windows were tinted, his truck was roomy, and they would have plenty of room and privacy to greet each other once she got into the truck. He rolled down his window as he pulled up and she opened her door. He called for her to get into his truck with him, and she did as he asked.

Everything about the next minute was surreal.

It felt, in Warren's heart, that God had basically rolled out some kind of metaphorical red carpet for Sasha to come to him. There was music playing, and there might as well have been lights and wind and glitter flying as she opened the door and smiled at him. She had on jeans and a sweatshirt, and her hair blew around wildly as the wind hit it.

She had dimples. She was a beauty, and Warren felt way more for her than he should at this point in their relationship. She had a look that was so sweet, and her smile was adorable.

"I'm nervous," she admitted sweetly, not seeming nervous at all.

Warren had protective, possessive thoughts. She had no idea what had just happened on the interstate. He knew he needed to slow down.

"You shouldn't be nervous."

He wanted to pull her onto his lap and start kissing her. She smelled like lemons and flowers, and Warren ached to have her closer to him.

"I can't believe you're here," she said, looking around. "This is a nice truck."

"Thank you. I can't believe you're in it," he said.

She took a deep breath and stared down shyly. He loved her profile. Her face was naturally round which gave her a sweet, adorable appearance. She was a cute little cupcake with sprinkles, and Warren felt like he wanted to cry at the sight of such an adorable gift. There was music playing on the radio, and he adjusted the volume, turning it up.

He closed his eyes and laid his hand, palm up, on the console. He wanted so badly to go ahead and touch her, and he couldn't think of a better way to do that than to stick out his hand and offer it to her.

His hand was only there for a few seconds before he felt her touch the center of it. He closed his hand around hers, gripping onto it. The music played. It was a song by a band he didn't know, but it was slow and the melody was nice. Her hand was in his, and he was electrified with the feeling of it. She was the woman he would marry. She was the one he would spend the rest of his life with. Now he just had to make sure she was on board with that.

For the moment, though, he would simply hold her hand. He would take in the feel of her—the smell. He brought her hand toward himself, smelling her wrist and letting her hand brush his cheek. He felt a surging sensation in his body and he clutched her hand to his chest as he slowly opened his eyes and regarded her.

Her dark eyes stared into his. She blinked and gave him a hint of a smile. Her lips. Her face. Warren was spellbound. He wondered how he had possibly found her. He had to find a way to be close to her on a regular basis. Memphis was too far from Nashville.

He cleared his throat. "Did you want to go inside and get something to eat?"

"Yeah, sure, that sounds good," she said, having no idea how in love he was in that moment.

Chapter 11

Sasha Faulkner

Warren did not have on his signature baseball cap. His hair was clean and combed back when I got in the truck, but it blew around wildly when he got out. It was thick and wavy—not as curly as mine. I was infatuated with Warren, and it was surreal that he seemed to feel the same about me. I glanced at him as we walked around the back of the truck to meet each other.

He smiled and held out his hand.

"They might know you in there," I said, nudging my head toward the restaurant.

I already hashed out my feelings on the subject. There were roughly ten or twelve people in plain sight when I walked into the restaurant earlier, and I figured Warren wouldn't want to be seen with me (or any woman) in public.

"What's that mean?" he said, still offering me his hand.

"You know. I mean, what if someone recognizes you?"

He tilted his head just slightly and shrugged. "I'm not that famous," he said. "The worst that could happen is that someone asks for a picture."

I thought about what would happen if Tori saw him in a restaurant.

"What?" he said when I hadn't moved to put my hand in his. "Even if they recognize me what's the big deal? Aren't musicians allowed to have a girlfriend?"

"You're too much," I said, shaking my head a little.

He reached out and took my hand, leading me into the restaurant. He was confident and sure of every step, and I walked next to him, holding his hand and feeling like I was in a music video.

It would be a miracle if I could eat. Food was the absolute last thought on my mind. I had it all built up that if we went somewhere together in public, we would keep a safe distance. His unrepentant proximity caused me to have the jitters. I turned to him before we made it to the door.

"I'm going to run to the restroom when we go in there," I said, even though I had already been once before. This was all happening so fast that I had to pause and take a second to breathe, wash my hands, and stare at myself in the mirror.

Warren nodded. I stared at the side of his face as we walked. I had always been short and curvy and August was tall and bony. People often asked if we were blood-related. Warren wasn't quite as tall as my brother, he was a just-above-average-size guy. But he was eight or nine inches taller than me, and I loved how he fit next to me.

"I'll go with you," he said. "To the men's room, I mean. That way we can sit down together."

We walked inside, and the lady at the counter greeted us. She told us that if we would be eating, we should seat ourselves when we were ready. I took a minute in the restroom to compose myself. I needed it. I liked Warren way too much. My feelings were getting all carried away. I looked at him, and I hoped for a future with him. He walked next to me, and in my mind, we might as well have been walking down the aisle.

I was too attached already, and told myself to calm down and take his 'girlfriend' statements for what they were—casual statements. He had said the G-word, though. He said it, I knew he had, and I still didn't believe it. He was the same Warren Manning I saw on the internet—the country outlaw who had thousands of fans singing along to his music at shows.

I dabbed my face with a damp paper towel and took a deep, calming breath. I didn't say it out loud, but inwardly I told myself that I was good enough. I pumped myself up, saying Warren would be lucky to have a girl like me.

I smiled at myself in the mirror. I had always been a confident person, but it turned out that trying to date a famous person could test one's self-esteem. I felt like I had worth as a person, and I knew I could be good to Warren, but the fact that he had such a large platform was just overwhelming. I had friends who had crushes on him, for goodness sake.

I found myself praying while I was in there. I said a prayer that God would please, please, please help Warren to fall madly in love with me, and the innocent prayer brought a smile to my face and brought me back to my childhood when I prayed that a guy named Preston Andrews would fall madly in love with me.

I smiled and shook my head at myself in the mirror as I asked God to forgive me for praying that same prayer from when I was a kid. I changed my prayer to the correct one of, *let Your will be done.* And then I added an addendum that I hoped His will included Warren.

I laughed at myself, and took off to meet Warren. He was just coming out of the men's room when I opened the door, and my smile broadened when I noticed him.

We found a booth nearby, and the same lady came over to check in on us. We gave her our drink orders and she dropped off the menus. I smiled at him after she walked away.

"I was thinking about camp," I said, out of nowhere. "I was in the bathroom, and I had this whole memory of one year as a kid when I went to camp."

I didn't mention Preston Andrews, obviously, or the prayer I had prayed.

"What kind of camp?" he said, looking interested.

"Church camp."

He regarded me. His stare was intense and his blue eyes were bright.

"Sasha, I realize I'm at risk of sounding too over-zealous, here, but could you… do you… what I'm trying to say is that I think I was supposed to meet you—like really supposed to."

I grinned at him. "I think so, too."

"I mean it, though," he said. "What made you think about church camp?"

"I don't know," I said, acting like I was searching my brain even though I knew. There was no way I would tell him I was in the restroom praying that I could marry him.

He put his hand on the table, and I slowly reached out and slid my hand in his, my gut aching and heart pounding.

"I don't care what made you say it," he said, staring straight into my eyes. "The timing of it is just amazing."

I smiled. "Why? Were you thinking about church camp?"

"I was, actually."

I thought at first that he was joking, but he held a serious expression.

"I was."

"Did you go to one?" I asked.

"Yes. Several. Every summer for a while."

"Me too, until my summers started being too full with theater stuff. Brandon, our old director, had camps for little kids all summer, and I started helping out with those."

"I stopped going once I went to high school," he said. "I was in my truck having all sorts of thoughts from back then—how going to those affected my music and my mindset—and then I come in here, and the first thing you talk about is church camp. It's just too good. Do you have a pen in your purse?"

"Yes, I do. Do you need it?"

"I do need it, please. And paper if you have it. I don't have my notebook."

I pulled my hand from his so that I could open and dig into the small, crossbody bag I had with me all the time. I knew the pen would be resting at the bottom, and I easily found it and brought it out, reaching across the table and handing it to him. He took it with a smile. Our eyes locked, and the color of his were just breathtaking.

"No paper, though," I said.

He grabbed a napkin from the table and began writing on it. He was hunched over, staring intently, and his eyes were fixed on what he was doing. I couldn't see the words, but I was aware that he was writing line after line of text. I felt transfixed, watching him. His eyebrows were furrowed and his gaze held steady on the napkin as he wrote.

He had just stopped writing and was staring at the words when the lady came up again. Warren put down the pen and folded the napkin, slipping it into his pocket.

"Would you like to hear a little more about our restaurant or our menu?" she asked.

"Sure, whatcha got?" he asked since we hadn't looked at the menus at all.

"Are you hungry for a sandwich or an entrée?" Warren glanced at me, and I shrugged with wide eyes.

"Sandwich is fine," I said.

"Sandwiches are good," he said to her.

"We've got a burger, a BLT, a chicken sandwich, a patty melt, a fish sandwich…" she blinked staring upward as if there were one she was missing.

"I'll have a burger," he said.

"Same," I agreed.

"Hamburger or cheeseburger?"

"Cheese," we both said at the same time.

She jotted something on her notepad and then asked us about side dishes. She picked up our menus and was about to take off, but she turned and hesitated near our table.

"You don't happen to be Warren Manning?"

"Yes, I do," Warren said with a slight grin and nod.

"I don't want to interrupt your dinner, but I just wanted to let you know that I love your music. I'm a big fan."

"Thank you so much."

"Would it be possible to get a picture on your way out?"

"Absolutely," Warren said.

She smiled like her day was made. "I'll get this order in," she said.

And then she took off. Warren put his hand on the table again, reaching out for me. I placed my hand in his.

"Was that a song?" I asked.

"Was what a song?"

"The napkin."

"Oh, yes."

He took his hand from mine long enough to push my pen across the table. "Thank you."

"Did you finish?" I asked.

He shrugged. "I got enough of it. I'll know what to do with it once I get home."

I stashed my pen, and he held his hand out again. It seemed as though he wanted to constantly touch me, which was so very welcome.

"Have you ever been to any other kind of camp?" he asked.

"I've been to lots of theater camps," I said. "I went to a couple of cooking camps and a sewing camp one time."

"I think you told me that," he said.

"What about you?" I asked him.

"No… no camps besides the ones I went to with friends—the church camps. My mom thought they were free, but looking back, I'm sure someone paid for me." He grinned thoughtfully, remembering. "I haven't thought about all this stuff in years."

"Me neither," I said. "Even my camp-counseling days kind of trailed off once I went to college and started working."

He sat up and adjusted his hand so that our hands were palm to palm and his fingers interlaced with mine. I did my best to take it all in because it was a moment I would try to relive a thousand times. The way he held onto me and stared at me—it was relentless, unapologetic.

Smitten was not the right word to describe what I felt. Our hands connected over the table, and it was as if we were in our own universe.

"Do you get recognized everywhere you go?"

"Not always. My cap's more of a giveaway when I have that on."

"But you don't have it on right now."

"I know, but we're right here in Tennessee. I have a lot of listeners around here. Sometimes, when I go out, I wear tinted glasses, but I don't mind taking a picture with her. She seems nice."

"Yeah, no, I was just wondering how much you can get out."

"I can do anything I want. There's never chaos or anything like that—unless I'm at a concert or something. But in my everyday life—I just live and function like a normal person."

"You're not normal, though, are you?" I asked staring at him. He squinted his blue eyes playfully at me.

"What's that supposed to mean?" he asked.

I shrugged a shoulder. "I don't know. That you're special."

"You're special," he said.

I patted my own chest—tiny little pats of self-satisfaction. "I am pretty special, aren't I?" I said making a face and pretending to be shy. I was being silly, and he knew it.

Chapter 12

Warren and I laughed and talked the whole time we were at the restaurant. There were a few people inside, but no one came up to us except for our server. The burgers were delicious, and I ate even though I wasn't hungry at all. I didn't want to seem like one of those girls who picked at my food on dates, so I ate even though I really felt like picking at my food. I was thankful it was tasty.

Our server brought us dessert on the house. We paid the check, and Warren took a picture with two people before we left. We had already talked about leaving in his truck to go to a park for a little while. We left my car in the parking lot of the restaurant and drove to a place I had already looked up. The parking lot had been wide open, and I welcomed the thought of a park with trees for shade.

Warren adjusted the console so that I could sit next to him on our way to the park. He left the engine running when we got there and locked the doors even though there was nobody around. I experienced a rush of excitement when he locked the truck doors. I knew he was simply trying to avoid any surprises and that it had nothing to do with trapping me in the vehicle, but it was fun to tell myself I was trapped.

"Are you kidnapping me in this truck?" I asked with a smile.

"Yes," he said. As he spoke, he adjusted in his seat and turned to me. I turned at the same time, and he pulled me in and kissed me. He was planning on doing it—the whole point of adjusting had been… this. His hand touched my jaw, urging me to look at him and… goodness. Warren didn't have to ask me twice. I leaned into him eagerly, letting my mouth press gently against his.

Our mouths were slightly open, and I could taste him. We had both taken a mint as we left the restaurant. I tasted the peppermint, and that combined with the feel of his warm mouth sent shockwaves through my body. I clutched a fistful of his shirt and urged him closer to me. He leaned in, but he kissed me lightly, letting his mouth, slightly open, rest on mine for no longer than a second or two at a time.

We kissed lightly several times before Warren pulled back to look at me. I ached to feel him kiss me again, but I didn't beg. I breathed a shaky breath and loosened my grip, and he leaned in and let his mouth touch mine again. I was out of my mind with desire when he pulled back.

"You're wonderful," he whispered.

I leaned in and kissed him again—a soft peck on the cheek to thank him for the compliment. He pulled back and stared at my face, holding the side of it, my cheek resting in his hand. I could feel where his fingertips were callused from playing the guitar. I noticed those rough edges when he held my hand, too, but I loved how it felt on the side of my face.

The cab of the truck was dimly lit because of his tinted windows, and I might as well have been in paradise right then with how perfect I felt.

And then right at the height of my elation, I felt a wave of guilt.

Tori.

I must have made a face because he said, "What?"

"You know that rule with friends… the one where you're not supposed to pursue someone if your friend is already in love with him? Well, I have this friend, Tori, who loves you. She's got you on her lockscreen and everything."

"You mentioned Tori to me before," he said, still staring sweetly at me.

"I did? Oh, gosh, well, I'm sitting in here, feeling like this is wonderful, and then I get a flash of your face on her phone. I don't know whether to feel guilty or jealous, or if I can just forget all those things and enjoy this moment for what it is."

"I think you answered your own question," he said.

"I did?"

"Yes."

"What did I say?"

He let out a little laugh. "You said you should forget all those things and enjoy this moment."

"I did say that."

He laughed again. "Yes, you did."

"Is it okay for me to do that?"

"Yes."

"What am I going to tell Tori?"

"That won't matter in the grand scheme of things."

"It won't?"

"No. Sasha… I know… I know we're not saying it yet, and we're not to that point, but I think… I'm pretty sure I love you. It's happening so naturally that I feel like I was just made to fall in love with you. Seeing you today, and having you here with me... it seems like we have to keep seeing each other moving forward."

"Oh, Warren, stop."

"What?"

I was breathless. "I can't take it. When you say things like that, it makes me feel all sorts of feelings."

"What feelings?"

"Like I need to rearrange my life to see you more."

"That's the exact type of feelings you need to be having."

"No, it's not. We live far away from each other. You travel with work, and I have school. The amount of time we can see each other is not mathematically adding up."

"Sasha?"

"Yeah?"

"Where are you right now, right this second?"

"I'm in your truck."

"Okay then. I think that's all the math we need for now. Can we try not to worry so much about the other days and just enjoy this one?"

"Yes, we can," I said, even though that was very difficult for me.

He let his lips touch mine again, and I was taken to another world.

"I want it more than you do, believe me," he whispered as he pulled back.

"What did you say?" I asked since I was so lost in his kiss that I didn't hear him.

"I said I want you with me every second," he said. "We'll figure out a way."

"I only have eight months of school left."

"Okay, we'll work it out. I leave tomorrow for a few weeks, most of October, but I was thinking maybe I can fly you out to Florida while I'm down there. Maybe you could see a show or two. I think I've got eight or ten shows lined up, and I would love for you to be at a few of them."

"You want me to go to Florida with you?"

"Yes."

"Next month?"

"Yes. Is that possible?"

"Sure," I said.

"I know you have school, but can you look into a long weekend?"

"Yes, I can," I said.

We stared at each other for what must have been a full minute. Our faces were only inches apart, the perfect distance for me to focus on his flawless features. His eyes were amazing, but in that silent minute, I looked at his nose and his jaw. His mouth made me weak in the knees. I had seen video of him singing, and I knew how it moved when he sang. It was unbelievable to me that the same mouth I had seen singing all those songs was right here in..."

I was in the middle of a thought when Warren pulled me into his lap. He adjusted his grip on me, and then he kissed me again, pulling me close. This time things were different. Warren kissed me passionately. The whole thing was urgent. He held me and kissed me, and his tongue slid against mine. His touch was gentle but scorching. My insides felt melted, and I moved, trying to get closer to him. I had to resist the urge to writhe, and so I just held onto fistfuls of his clothing for dear life while he kissed me. The exchange was not casual at all. There was barely restrained passion taking place. The music played, and I couldn't even hear it over the pounding of my own heart. I was enthralled, entranced, enraptured.

Warren made his feelings clear with that kiss.

I felt claimed and utterly spent when he finally pulled back. I shivered, curling into him. He held me, hugging me against his chest.

He cleared his throat. "You're my girl, okay?"

My head rested on his chest, and the sound of his voice sounded deep and soft. "I want to be," I said.

"You are."

"I thought about telling my brother."

"Please tell your brother. I'll call your brother and tell him right now."

I laughed at the thought of that.

"I will. Does he know you're talking to me at all?"

"No. No one in my life does."

"It's okay, Sasha. You don't have to be scared that I have a few fans. I'm sure your family's not going to go make a commercial about it… and even if they do… whatever. I don't care if you tell your family about us. I want you to."

I wanted to ask him how many people I could tell, because if I told a few people at Memphis Players or at school, word would get out, and people would start to ask me questions about it. I didn't say any of that to him. It was silly for me to care so much about defining our relationship. I knew I could tell August and a few others without anything getting out.

"And I've got to tell people in my life about you," he said. "We'll need to hook you up with Becky so she can help you make travel plans."

"Becky's your assistant."

"Yes," he said. "And it's going to be obvious to Jared and all my road crew that you're with me when you come see us on the road. Everyone will know then."

"I just worry about your fans—people like Tori. I don't want them to get their feelings hurt."

"I love what you just said."

"You do? What do you love about it?"

"I love that you're sweet enough to even think like that and worry about my fans."

"I am a fan. I can't wait to hear you sing live."

"You can hear me anytime."

"Really? You'll sing for me?"

"Only if you sing for me."

"No way," I said.

"Why not? You do musicals."

"Because singing is the world where I'm second, third, fourth best. I can act, and I can even dance, but singing… I've always struggled with that part of it the most while doing musicals. It's not that I struggle, necessarily, but I'm not the best over there. I'm the third or fourth best, usually. So, it's hard to think about showing you that aspect of myself. I want to show you all the stuff I'm best at—like sudoku."

He laughed and held me close. "How about we can start with dancing and work our way to singing? I'm not going to make it without your dancing."

"Dancing's no problem," I said. "I'd love to dance with you."

"What about for me?"

"I'd love to do that, too," I said.

We started talking about all the places he was going on this short tour. It included six Florida cities, and we talked about which ones might be a possibility for me to visit. That made us talk about other Florida things, which somehow got us talking about movies. I rested next to him, snuggling comfortably into his embrace. More than an hour passed in what felt like a minute, and then suddenly it was time for us to go our separate ways.

Warren mentioned having to get back to Nashville, and I sat up to say goodbye even though it was the very last thing I wanted to do. Warren shifted when I moved, and I stared at him. Our eyes met, and he kissed me again. It had been a while since our mouths met. The taste of the mint had faded, and I tasted Warren instead, and it was amazing. I almost melted when he opened his mouth and kissed me deeply. It all happened too quickly, and before I knew it, he was pulling back. Both of us were breathing deeply from the quick burst of passion.

"Sash, we have to get on the road."

It was obvious by his tone that he wasn't happy about it at all.

"Let's plan a trip. Maybe even sooner than Miami. We'll look at Tampa."

"Okay," I said, adjusting in my seat to give him room to drive.

He kissed me one time before he took off. Warren was such a man. He handled life well, and he didn't hesitate. I felt confident and sure sitting next to him. He rested his hand protectively on my thigh as he drove back to the restaurant to drop me off at my car.

Chapter 13

Two weeks later

Auditions for the Memphis Players winter show were happening now. They had changed formats with the new director, and now there were only two shows a year—one set of auditions was in October for the show in February, and the other auditions were in April for a show in August.

Because of newly-formed connections with the Fairchild family, all shows were now held at the Blackbird Theater, the same place where Bailey and Ryan had gotten married. The troop still rehearsed at Hillsdale High, but all shows were held at the Blackbird.

The winter show was going to be The Addams Family Musical. It was a cute show that I had been in years ago, and I would enjoy doing it, but I just couldn't fit it in—not with trying to ace my last two semesters of college and build a relationship with Warren. My plate was already too full as it was.

I did, however, want to go to auditions. The first round of auditions was being held on Friday afternoon. The last one was scheduled for 8pm, and then Abe (the new director) had to tackle the task of casting. He and his team would post a callback list by midnight, and everyone who was considered for a principle role would be expected to meet at the high school the following morning at 8am.

I would be there for all of it. I didn't have anything going on with school, and it was easy enough for me to switch shifts with someone and get off of work. Tori was the assistant director, and she had called to ask me to be there some and help the team during the audition weekend even though I wasn't planning on doing the show. I easily agreed. I wanted to see how it went with August and all of my friends, and I loved being around the whole process. I probably would have still come to the auditions even if Tori hadn't asked me to.

Quite a few people were already in the school auditorium when I arrived. There were over sixty people auditioning, and they had been assigned times. We had been used to a certain thing with Brandon, our old director, and Abe did things differently. He was young and determined, and he did everything with slightly more intensity than Brandon. I liked his style, though, and all of us felt lucky to have him.

West Side Story was his first show as director, and he had settled in nicely. He came from New York City and he had done some big things there as an actor. We all welcomed him from the start.

There were always new people with questions, and Tori had me running interference for the directors and answering questions. I also did things like get people drinks or whatever else they needed. I was volunteering my time, but I didn't mind at all. It was a small price to pay to be there with everyone and get to see them compete for roles.

Stage productions were like nothing else I had ever experienced in life. They were each their own living organism. Starting on day one, at auditions, each show had its own feel, its own life. There were different characters and songs, and a different cast each time. Many of the same people auditioned time and again, but every show felt completely different.

I loved being a part of it all, but being there today was convenient for another reason altogether. Today I would tell Tori, and probably some others, about my relationship with Warren. August knew about it, and so did my parents, but I hadn't told a single friend.

Things were all coming down to the wire, though, and I had to say something. In less than a week, I would go to Florida to meet Warren. People in my life would start noticing something now that I was going out of town.

I had six days before my trip, and I absolutely could not wait. He and I had talked for hours and hours on the phone, but we had not used Facetime, and I hadn't seen his face in weeks. It would feel so good to finally have him in front of me.

But boy, did we talk. We had so much fun talking about everything. I loved to know his opinions, and most of the time they lined up with mine. He shared songs with me. He sang to me. I loved him and he loved me, and neither of us cared that it was all really sudden. In these last days and weeks, I had built something with Warren that was deeper than the initial feelings of attraction.

We said funny, weird things to each other, and we told embarrassing stories from our childhood. I knew how I felt about Warren. We felt established. We didn't spend our time defining our relationship, but in my heart, I knew that he loved me and had no desire to be with anyone else. It was surreal to think about, but I felt confident in it. Warren made me feel that way. He was good to me. He called me his honeybee because he said I reminded him of a little bee dancing around the store that first day.

I had developed so many new feelings for him that it was difficult for me to rewind and get back to the point where I should've let Tori and my other friends know about it. It was odd that I had kept it from my circle of friends, but I didn't know how to tell them and one day led to another, and now there I was, hanging out with all of them six days before I would leave town on trip to go see Warren. I didn't know what to say to bring it up, so I just kept avoiding it. We went through the first hour of auditions, and then we took a short break.

"Could you run to my car with me?" Tori asked, leaning over to look at me.

"Sure," I said.

My heart started pounding right when she said it. I had been looking for an opportunity to spend a minute alone with Tori, and I had the feeling this was it. I wanted to tell her first. She knew that I knew she liked Warren, and she would want to hear this information from me first. My thoughts became scrambled as I stood up from the auditorium chair and began to follow Tori.

"I have some of Kennedy's clothes in my car, and I didn't want to go out to the parking lot alone," she explained as we walked down the aisle.

I just smiled and nodded because I was too busy getting my thoughts together to do anything else.

"I love Warren Manning," I said.

I regretted saying it before it even came out of my mouth, and because of this, my words came out more of a slow, drunken-sounding mess.

"You? Are you into Warren Manning now?"

"Yes."

"I told you he's good. Now I bet you regret giving him the pencil that night." She laughed.

Other people were all around us, and I couldn't get myself together enough to have this conversation in front of all of them. My thinking was delayed several seconds.

Tori continued to laugh in a nostalgic tone like she was thinking of something. "You may love him, but I actually *told him* I love him," she said.

I looked at her, feeling mortified but only coming up with a questioning expression.

"It was at a concert, and everything got quiet for a second. Everyone had just been yelling, but they got quiet, and right before he started to speak, I yelled out. I said *'I love you, Warren!'* and he heard me! I know he heard me because he said 'I love you too' before he started talking again. Can you believe it? You couldn't appreciate that story a few months ago when you had never heard of him."

"No, I actually like him for real," I said.

We were now walking in the halls of the high school on our way to the exit. Everything was happening so fast that I couldn't think of a better way to say what I was feeling.

Tori laughed. "I told you, he's good," she said.

"No, I've been talking to him. Not the singer, Warren, but the regular guy. I mean, he is the singer, too, but I've been talking to the regular guy. We, we talk all the time. I'm just about to go down to Florida to a gig where he's playing."

"You're going all the way to Florida to see Warren Manning?" she asked, still not getting it. "Are you flying, or driving?"

"I'm flying," I said. "He bought the ticket."

She smiled at me. "Sure, he did. Can you get him to buy me one, too?" she asked, pretending.

I was on her right so I held the door while we stepped outside, walking toward her car. "No, I'm being serious. Warren and I are talking in real life. He bought the ticket, for real."

She stared at me, seeming to suddenly understand that I was trying to have a sincere conversation. We still walked slowly toward her car, but she kept her eyes trained on me, looking at me. She seemed to understand a little more, but she was still making an expression that made it look like she was expecting me to say I'm joking.

"What do you mean, you're talking?"

"We talk. We're romantic. We're dating or whatever."

She let out a coughing, scoffing laugh, stumbling as we went through the parking lot. "You are so totally joking," she said.

"No, I'm actually not," I said, looking injured.

She saw my expression when she glanced at me and her own expression turned to one of confusion.

"Is it so hard to believe that Warren Manning would like someone like me?" I asked.

"No, Sasha it's not. It's just hard to believe that he does like you. Are you even serious right now?"

"I actually am."

"You're telling me you're dating Warren Manning?" she said in a disbelieving tone.

"Yes."

"Do you have his number on your phone?"

"Yes. Yes, Tori."

"You have Warren Manning's phone number?"

"Yes."

She stopped walking when we reached her car. She stared straight at me. "Call him," she said.

"What?"

"Call him. If you have his number, call him and show me what you're talking about."

"Are you not going to believe me otherwise?"

"No, I believe you," she said easily.

I could tell she was lying, that she seriously wanted me to call him.

"I just would love to hear his voice come out of your phone."

I wanted to prove her wrong so badly that I didn't consider it to be out-of-line for her to ask me. Maybe I would look back on it later and regret it, but in the moment, I took my phone out of my back pocket and began dialing Warren's number. I put the phone to my ear.

"Hey my honeybee," he said, picking up the phone. "I thought you were busy today."

He was not on speaker, but Tori could hear a male voice. I knew because of the way her eyebrows furrowed.

"Are you busy?" I asked.

"No, I'm driving."

"I'm here with my friend," I said, warning him not to say too much. "My friend, Tori, is right here, and she's a big fan of yours. We have to get back inside. We only have a second, but I'm going to put you on speakerphone so you can say 'hi' to her for two seconds."

"Hey, Tori."

"Hello," she said, leaning stiffly toward the phone.

"Hey, Tori, Sasha told me you've come to see me three times in concert."

"I have," she said, choking out the words and trying to sound casual. She regarded me with wide eyes.

"Thank you," he said. "I'm always thankful when people take time out of their lives to come see me play. Sash said you traveled, too."

"Yeah, because you've never play in Memphis. Except when you show up at a dive bar, which I'm never lucky enough to be there on the right day."

"Thanks for being so good to Sasha. She really loves all of her theater friends."

"Oh, yeah, no, we love Sasha," she said staring at me with an absolutely stunned expression.

"Okay," I said, cutting in. I took it off speaker phone and put the phone to my ear. "Thank you. I'll call you later," I said to him.

"All right call me when you get home tonight."

"I will," I said. "Talk to you soon."

"Yep," he agreed.

We hung up and I looked at Tori.

"That seriously sounded like Warren Manning," she said, smiling a little. She was blushing and starting to sweat a little, and I knew deep down she knew it was him.

"It was Warren Manning. I told you we met at Kramer's."

I expected her to bend down and get whatever she needed from her car, but she didn't. She just stood there, looking blank, stupefied, staring into the car with the door open.

"I didn't know he was famous when we met. I knew his name was Warren, but I didn't know he was a singer."

I started to say that he had gotten in touch with me about the Valentine song, but I didn't mention it. I figured this was enough information for now.

"And what happened?"

"I don't know. We started talking. He still doesn't seem famous to me."

Tori was nervous and distracted. She reached down and got a bundle of clothes out of her car and then stood with a sigh.

"Are you being serious right now, Sasha?" she asked.

"Of course, I'm being serious. You just talked to Warren on the phone."

"That could've been your brother, impersonating him. I didn't even see what number you dialed."

"I promise it wasn't August. He's inside right now. I wouldn't do that to you. I was nervous about telling you about Warren because I knew you liked him as a singer or whatever."

"I do like him as a singer or whatever," she said. There was a little biting edge to her tone, and it made me feel defensive.

We started walking back toward the auditorium. We knew we had to. There was no time to waste, and both of us knew it.

"I'm sorry, but I can't even comprehend what you're telling me," she said. "You said you're going to see Warren in Florida, and you said he paid for your plane ticket." She made the statement as if something didn't quite add up.

"Yes, I did say that."

"Warren Manning bought you a plane ticket?"

"Yes," I said, even though now I regretted telling her that fact.

Chapter 14

Four days later

"I heard Warren Manning bought you a plane ticket for Florida," Gina said when she called me a few days later.

I was at my apartment and had just finished helping my roommate study for her biology test. I was happy to hear from Gina. The cast list for Addams family had just come out the night before, and Gina was cast as Wednesday Addams. It was a role she was excited about, and I thought she would be calling me about that. I didn't dream the first words out of her mouth would be to ask about Warren and my flight arrangements.

"Tori's the only person I told," I said, shaking my head and smiling.

"She told me," Gina said.

I laughed. "I thought you would want to talk about the cast list."

"I do. I'm excited. I got your text. That was really sweet. Thank you. I'm pumped about Wednesday. I was calling to ask you about that plane ticket, though. I'm mainly interested in it because if you didn't have to pay for that ticket, then you can use the money for something else."

"For what? Do you need money for something?"

"No, no but you do. I want you to go on a spa day before your trip, and you need money for it. You're going to need about two-fifty or three hundred. Can you do that? I wish I had enough to pay for it, but I don't. I can make the arrangements. Do you have any money saved? Can you ask your parents for that much, maybe?"

"What arrangements? What's this for exactly?"

"We have to get you all fixed up if you're going to see Warren Manning. We have to get your hair, nails, and maybe eyebrows done. I guess we'll skip a facial, and I hope you have some outfits you can put together, because the budget I mentioned is just for hair and nails—that's not for new clothes."

"I have literally never had any of that stuff done before, hair and nails, I mean. My aunt cuts my hair at her house."

"I know, Sasha. I've been to your aunt's with you before, remember? She has the boxer."

"Rosco."

"Yeah, I know you've never had that stuff done before. That's what makes it fun."

"Are you trying to find a nice way to say I'm gross and I need grooming before I go see Warren?"

"No. And we're all gross. You're not gross. It's just fun to get extra dolled up."

"You're right, it would be fun. Let me think about it."

"Don't think too long. I need to get an appointment."

"Are you coming with me?"

"I'll go with you, but I'm not getting anything done. I just got my hair done like two weeks ago."

"You don't have to come with me, but you can go ahead and make the appointment," I said. "Is it with your hair person?"

"Yes. Allie. She's amazing."

"I know. I always love your hair. I don't think I want color or anything, though. And no big changes."

"Yeah, it'll be fine. She knows how to put on some kind of gloss-color thing. She'll get you all fixed up."

"You're so sweet," I said. "When is this?"

"Tomorrow. And we're going to do your nails while we're there. They have a girl who does manicures, too."

"Nails? Fake?"

"Yeah, but not long ones. They're natural."

"Am I going to like that?"

"Yes, of course. She knows how to do it. You'll love it. It'll make you feel like a princess."

"You're amazing, Gina."

"It wasn't just me. I schemed it with your other friends, too. I'm just the one who called because I know a hair girl."

"Who talked about this with you?"

"Tori was there."

"Wh-she was? What'd she say?"

Gina laughed. "I knew you'd be worried about Tori. She's obsessed with Warren, but it's not like that. She's happy for you."

"That makes me feel good because she didn't talk to me much after I told her."

"She's fine," Gina said. "We were all talking about it today, and we were all excited for you. Tori was in on it. We all wanted you to have a spa day."

"Thank you for mentioning it to me," I said. "And for getting the appointment."

"I am not sure that I'll be able to do it, but I'm going to give it a shot. I'll text you back in just a minute to confirm."

"You're amazing, Gina. Thank you."

"You're welcome. I'm going by there if you get an appointment. I think it will be fun."

"I want you to. I don't even know how to use those kinds of places. Is it fine for me to walk in the door and just tell them my name?"

"That's all you would have to do, but I will try to come. Let me call her and see what time. Can you go Thursday if tomorrow doesn't work?"

"No. My flight leaves Thursday afternoon."

"Okay, tomorrow it is. Tomorrow or nothing."

"Yes. Thank you, Gina."

"Thank me later. I have to call Allie and see what's up with her schedule. I'll let you know in a minute."

We hung up and I went to my bathroom to look at myself in the mirror. I had dark hair, and I had often thought of adding highlights. I didn't know or care what she did with my hair. Gina always looked so nice, and I trusted her hair person.

I was excited at the thought of professional help with my appearance. I had made it by okay on my own—my mom was fashionable enough, and I had learned some things on the internet, but the thought of a spa day made me more and more excited by the minute. I turned on music and danced while I waited for her to text me back.

I had been dancing a lot lately for two reasons. One because I had a ton of nervous energy about my upcoming trip, and two because I had been practicing a dance for Warren. I planned a three-minute segment and set it to the Clash song, of course. I wasn't trying to be provocative. It wasn't that kind of dance. It was lighthearted and fun, and I knew Warren would appreciate it. I planned to perform it for him in Tampa, sometime when we had a quiet moment at the hotel.

I heard from Gina within minutes, and she confirmed that Allie could see me at 9am the following morning. I would have to get someone to cover my shift at the chocolate shop, but I could make that happen.

I went over the dance again that night. I didn't need the practice since I had it down, but I was excited and pumped about my hair appointment, so I danced for fun.

Allie and Gina made it easy for me the next day. Gina knew I wanted to keep the changes mellow, and the two of them made all the decisions for me. Allie applied about twenty foils in my hair and some sort of all-over gloss color on the hair that wasn't in foils. It came out amazing. It was basically my own hair color but different, richer, better. She trimmed it also. It was shoulder-length with enough layers to give it some shape. The base was richer than my natural color with a few understated highlights. She shaped my eyebrows and removed all the other unwanted facial hair from my face.

I also had some beautiful, natural-looking nails, thanks to a woman named Harmony who tended to my nails on a rolling cart while I was under the hair dryer. They were shiny and perfect.

Allie styled my hair, and I left that place three hours later, feeling like a million bucks. It was more like three-hundred-and-twenty dollars, but I had a few products to take home and a healthy glow, and it was well worth it. I didn’t go around blowing that amount of money on a regular basis, but this was a special occasion, and I didn't regret it at all.

I didn't do any shopping for clothes, but I owned some outfits I liked. I packed my lotions and perfumes. I packed makeup, hair products, clothes, and undergarments. I packed enough for eight days even though I was only staying for three.

I was so excited to see Warren that I did all sorts of beauty regimens that I wasn't used to. I might as well have been taking baths in rose petals for the last three days. I used bath bombs and did facial scrubs and things I didn't normally do. I wasn't a changed person or anything, but I had insanely good hygiene at the moment, which was great because I had a three-and-a-half-hour flight and now it was late.

I lost an hour with the change in time zone, and I had to find my ride, so it was 10pm when I made it to the hotel. I would meet Warren and Jared there. Jared was a close friend from Nashville who basically lived with Warren.

Jared had a job he could do from his laptop, so he had been traveling with Warren for the last few years. Technically, he had his own apartment, but he was with Warren a lot. He was a handy guy to have around, and they had a lowkey friendship where they could just be quiet and exist in front of each other. I knew all about him already and had even communicated with him via text.

They originally met in a bar where Warren was trying to get a gig before he got famous. Jared was managing the place and hired Warren to play. They made a connection then, and had been friends ever since. The two of them always shared a suite, and Jared acted as a bodyguard type who ran interference if Warren had persistent fans.

Warren reserved me the room right next door to theirs, and I had no problem finding it. The driver and the concierge at the hotel had made everything really easy for me. I just gave them my name, and I was taken to exactly the right places.

Warren had texted me earlier to let me know that he would arrive at the hotel soon after me, so I was anxious to get settled and cleaned up. There was a bouquet of tropical flowers waiting in my room along with a note that said, *I can't wait to see you!* The paper smelled like Warren. It had come out of his notebook—the one he often carried to jot down lyrics. I could imagine him as he wrote this and put it here. I could picture his face—envision that white smile underneath that baseball cap. This whole relationship still felt surreal.

I had traveled before, but my family didn't make a regular habit of it. It was certainly the first time I had traveled alone, and my body pulsed with excitement as I stood in the hotel room with the view and the flowers. It was late, but I was so full of adrenaline that I felt like I could stay up for hours and hours.

I texted my family with a selfie to let them know that I was safe. My mom and dad had been convinced that I would get kidnapped before I managed to make it to Florida, so I knew they would be happy to get an update. Afterward, I went to the bathroom to check it out and freshen up. I washed my hands and sprayed some of my favorite perfume. I wiped my face a little, too, and reapplied a little foundation and lip balm.

I played music over my phone speaker, but I kept thinking about another song. Warren was planning on singing *Somebody Else's Valentine* at his concert tomorrow night. He hadn't released it yet, but he had already been performing it live, and I knew he would play it at the concert the following evening. I had never heard him play it live before, and it was surreal because I was the girl in the song. Warren Manning wrote a love song, and it was about me. I stared at myself in the mirror, standing up straight and putting my shoulders back, working up the courage to be that girl. I reminded myself that Warren already liked me for who I was—I didn't have to work at it. I could be myself and be natural and things would work out.

Warren had been busy, but I knew he planned to be home by eleven. I heard a knock on my door, and I grinned when I looked at the time and noticed he was early. I took a deep breath and a last glance of myself in the mirror before heading to the door. A quick glance into the peephole, and I saw a fisheye version of Warren standing there. I was so excited that I forgot to breathe.

I swung open the door, smiling widely the second I laid eyes on him. He opened his arms, and I walked into them. I smiled uncontrollably as I squeezed him tightly. My eyes were closed for a second, but I pulled away, stepping back when I opened them and realized we weren't alone.

"Hey Jared, I didn't see you standing there."

"It's okay," Warren said, keeping his hand on my side, holding me close.

I stuck out my hand to shake Jared's. I had seen his picture. I had heard all about him, and even talked to him on the phone a time or two. But this was our first time to meet.

Chapter 15

My brother and I had been extremely close since we were kids. I was close to my dad, too, and some other guys. I was used to having guys around. As far as hanging out with the bros went, I was good at it—at least as good as my brother. He liked things like books and theater, and I liked sports more than he did. I kept up with a lot of professional athletes, and I was able to talk about the latest in sports news.

All this to say, I knew I would get along well with Warren's best friend, Jared, and I most certainly did. He was funny and cool, and the three of us hung out and talked in the living room for at least three hours that night. They didn't have to be at the gig until 5pm the following day, and they seemed like they were in no hurry to go to bed.

At one point in the conversation, we started talking about food, and that prompted us to call room service. We ordered a meal and dessert, and we sat in the living room of their suite, laughing and talking and having the best time.

I made a real effort to get along with Jared because I knew they had been friends for a long time, and I didn't want Jared to think that I was trying to come between him and Warren. I didn't want Warren to think that either.

It happened effortlessly, though. Jared was a really cool person, and I could definitely understand why Warren wanted him around all the time. He was smart and funny, and he knew when to be quiet. He was the perfect sidekick type, talking Warren up and helping him out. He also seemed happy to have me there. Warren and I hadn't gone crazy with the PDA, but we had made some contact during the evening, and Jared didn't look twice or give Warren any sort of hard time about it.

He had just walked into the kitchen when Warren reached out for my hand. We had been sitting next to each other, but this was the first time we touched since we ate. I made eye contact with him—those blue eyes taking me off-guard no matter how many times I glanced at them. I wondered when the newness would wear off. I wondered when I would stop marveling. They were just so blue.

"I want to see that dance," Warren said.

I had told Warren about my dance earlier when Jared went to use the restroom. I scrunched my face at him, and he laughed. All I had said before was that I had a dance to show him, so he truly had no idea what I was talking about.

"I am not doing that in front of Jared," I said.

Warren furrowed his eyebrows at me. "Is it private?" he asked, teasing me.

"No, no, it's definitely not… I mean, it's funny, if anything. One of my friends helped me with it, Gina. It's just a little number that I set to that song."

"What song?"

"That Clash song."

"Really?" he said, a bright smile flashing across his face.

"Yes."

"Do it for me."

"Now?"

"Yes. I'm fine with Jared seeing it if it's just something you and your friend made up. He'd like it."

"I'll do it if you want me to," I said, feeling shy, but wanting to make him proud.

Warren told Jared I was going to show them something I made up with my friend. I started to play the song, and Warren did it on his phone instead so that he could connect to the built-in speakers. I played a planned version of air guitar for that familiar first guitar lick, and then I went into the dance number that I had created and rehearsed. I knew it so well, that my body found the beat easily. I did every step, and I had fun doing it.

The song itself was easy to enjoy, the sound system was booming, and I got lost in the routine, smiling at them and posing when it was finished.

The boys yelled, clapped, and asked me to do it again. I, of course, refused. I was winded, and I jogged to the kitchen to get myself some water. I knew there were some bottles in the fridge.

"I'm getting water!" I shouted, assuming they'd go on conversing without me.

My heart was still pounding and my breathing was heavy from all the dancing. I stuck my head in the fridge, smiling at the fact that it was cool and felt good on my skin, but I was also smiling because I was imagining the look on Warren's face as he was watching me. I was grinning at the thought of it when I felt and heard him come up behind me.

I stood up straight, turning to regard him. Jared was in the living room, and we were being blocked by the fridge door, so Warren leaned in and kissed me. I felt the gentle, quick contact of his lips on mine, and I held my breath even though I hadn't fully caught it.

"Hi," I whispered when he pulled back.

"How's my bee?"

"Good," I said, smiling.

His gaze scanned my face. "I don't know what Jared's doing, or how late he's staying up."

"I need to go, anyway," I said. "It's late."

"I'm mad at myself for saying he could watch that dance," he said, whispering.

"Why?"

"Because it was too good," he said. "I should have kept it for myself." His face was close to mine, and I couldn't take it.

"Don't worry, I'll make up more for you," I said quietly. I could see how Warren was looking at me. He liked my dancing. I would even go so far as to say he loved it. He took a deep breath, and his chest rose. He licked his lips, and I thought I might die. I nudged my chin upward a little and he kissed me again—a quick one on the side of my mouth.

"It's late, I need to go," I said.

Warren made a disappointed face and let out a little sigh.

"Can you walk me to my room so we can get a second?" I whispered.

"I most certainly can," he said. "Do you have to leave now?"

I sighed deeply, finally calming my breathing from the dance. "I should," I said. "You have to play tomorrow, and it's late."

"When can I see you again?"

"Right now. You're seeing me right now."

"I mean tomorrow," he said.

"Oh, whatever time. I'm sure I will be up before you. When I'm traveling, I usually wake up by eight or so no matter how late I stay up."

I took a sip of the bottled water and offered it to him. He refused with a little shake of the head and I took another sip. We stared at each other. The fridge door was open this whole time.

"I don't know why he's still up," Warren whispered.

"It's fine. I should go, anyway."

Warren moved to close the door while I moved out of the way, casually taking a sip of water and trying to make it look like I wasn't all wound up. I glanced into the living room area to find that Jared was not only there, he was looking our way. I gave him a little smile and turned to look at Warren.

"I'm so glad you're here," he said quietly, taking hold of my hand as we stood next to each other.

"I'm happy, too," I answered in the same tone.

"I love you," he said.

He said it.

We had done a lot of talking on the phone. A lot. Hours and hours. But we had never said that. We had never even hinted at it. I was certainly not expecting it, in that moment, with Jared right there in the next room.

"You do?" I asked, whispering shyly and looking up at him.

"Yes."

I hesitated for a second or two and then made a playful but defensive expression at him. "Well, I had no idea. This is great. Are you waiting to hear from me?" I was being funny and playful even though my insides were completely melted. It was an absolute wonder that I was standing upright at all. I felt like I didn't have bones. Warren had just told me he loved me. He had looked me in the face and said it, point blank.

"I am waiting to hear it, but you can tell me later."

Jared moaned as he stood up, and I glanced that way. He lifted the bottom of his shirt up, stretching and rubbing his own stomach. He spent a ton of time in the gym. Both of them did. I only glanced that way for a second, but it was long enough to see Jared's exposed torso.

"I should go," I said, speaking louder.

"I'm walking Sasha to her room," Warren said, holding onto my hand.

"Okay," Jared said. "Night Sasha. That dance was fire, girl."

"I told her that," Warren said. "She's amazing."

"Yes, sirrr, I guess this is goodnight to the fair lady. It's been an absolute pleasure. I guess I'll be seeing you in the morning."

I smiled at Jared. "That sounds great, thank you. I had fun tonight, too."

"Even though you got devastated at quarters?"

We didn't drink, but we played several rounds of the drinking game where you try to get a quarter to land in a juice glass by bouncing it on a table first. I had never tried it before, and I was bad at it. I made it in less than half the time, and the boys could do it consistently. I didn't care, and I had been acting silly with them. I narrowed my eyes playfully at Jared for bringing it up.

"I'll practice and get you next time," I said, pointing at him.

"Please do," he said, teasing me. "Go ahead and try."

Jared headed into his bedroom just as Warren and I left the suite—all of us saying goodnight to each other. My room was technically right next door to theirs, but we had to walk down the hall to get there.

"I get to see you in concert tomorrow night," I said as we walked. "I better get a ticket."

"Did you not get a ticket?" he asked, squinting at me like he was serious.

"No, I didn't," I said, pretending I thought he was serious, too.

Warren shook his head doubtfully. "Ooh, I'm really not sure if you're going to be able to get one this late. It's a smaller venue than I normally play. I think it might be sold out."

"Is it really sold out?" I asked, being serious and glancing at him.

We hesitated by my door, and I took the keycard out of my back pocket and scanned it absentmindedly. I heard it click and turned the knob, and Warren grinned at me.

"It is sold out, but that doesn't apply to you."

"I knew you were joking, but I didn't realize it was sold out. That's so cool. I'm oblivious since I don't do much social media."

"Becky doesn't put that kind of stuff on my social media, anyway. I don't know, now that I think about it, maybe she does. I really don't know what she puts on there."

We stepped inside, and he took me into his arms with a smile.

"I was just messing around, anyway. A ticket is irrelevant for you. I didn't even think about a seat. I figured you'd be backstage. You can watch from the side, or go wherever you want. Everybody will know you're with me."

I smiled up at him, and he adjusted with me in his arms. The door was closed, and we had privacy, but he didn't come past the entryway.

"I'm stuck on what you said." I bit my lip after I spoke, feeling shy about bringing it up.

"Oh, are you talking about a few minutes ago, in my hotel room, when I looked at you and told you that I loved you?"

"Y-yes I was," I cleared my throat before continuing. "I was talking about that."

He held my face in his hands, studying me, staring straight at me from whatever the distance of perfection was… maybe seven inches. "I love you, Sasha. Je t'aime. That's the only other language I know it in, or I'd say it all the ways. There's also amor, but I don't know the phrase. I love you. I love everything about you. I want you to know I've never felt like this. It's love. There's nothing else it could be."

I wanted to cry, but I desperately held it in, blinking past my burning stinging eyes. I had a lump in my throat. He meant the words that were coming out of his mouth, and those words happened to be glorious. Warren kissed me after that. He kissed me like it was the first time we admitted we loved each other. I didn't say the words, I didn't have time. But I kissed him back, and it was completely obvious, based on this kiss, that we were two people who were in love. We didn't just kiss, we connected, we communicated physically. We spent several long minutes in that entryway, getting to know each other in a way we never had before. There was lots of staring at each other between kisses, but we never said a thing.

I was in such a state of love and bliss that it was impossible to tell how much time had passed. I thought it might be less than an hour… but there was just no way to be sure.

Warren gave me a regretful smile as he pulled back. "I have to go," he said finally.

"I know. It's never going to feel like a good time to say goodnight."

"Never, ever," he agreed.

"But goodnight, anyway."

He flashed me that devastating half-grin. "Goodnight, Sasha."

Chapter 16

I was on cloud nine. I was way past there, actually, cloud eleven, cloud twenty-seven, perhaps. I was elated, smitten, overjoyed, ecstatic. I could not wipe a smile off of my face, even though I was alone. It was late, and I had taken a shower right after Warren left my room. I knew I needed one, and I knew I should go to bed, but the excitement was too much, and I couldn't imagine falling asleep at the moment.

The three of us had talked and laughed so much tonight that my face hurt, and there I was, still smiling at the thoughts and memories. In this moment, I was more content than I had ever been in my entire life. It was an amazing feeling. I turned the television on for background light, but I didn't pay attention to it. I knew finding sleep would be a challenge, but I sat on the bed so that I could try to get myself to settle down.

I had only been sitting there for a few minutes when my phone lit up and buzzed. I looked down to find Jared's name on my screen. I had his number saved because he had helped with some of my travel arrangements.

I opened the screen and read the text right away.

Jared:

You up?

My instant thought was to be concerned, and I started typing.

Me:
Yes. Is everything okay?

Jared:
Yes, can I come next door and talk to you for a second? It's about Warren.

Me:
Of course.

My heart began beating faster because I was already fearing the worst. I waited on pins and needles, and it was just a moment later when I heard a couple of knocks on my door. I opened it, staring out at Jared, standing there, wanting him to spill his guts instantly. He just smiled. My eyes widened when he didn't open his mouth first thing.

"You don't have on any makeup."

That was the last thing I expected him to say, and I flinched. "Yeah, I know. I took a shower. Is everything okay?"

"Yeah, no, you look good. I just wanted to talk to you about a few things, but it's going to take longer than a second. Can I come inside, just for a minute?" He peeked around me, looking inside.

"You have a couch in here, don't you? Is there any way I can come inside for a minute?"

He seemed a little worried, and of course, I invited him inside. I couldn't wait to hear what he had to say, and I stared at him expectantly the whole time we sat down. Jared didn't look at me. He leaned over and sighed, putting his face in his hands, looking upset.

"You're scaring me," I said.

"Oh, no, I'm sorry," he said, glancing at me. "I just don't even know where to begin. I'm having a really hard time, here. It's something I've never dealt with before, so I'm trying to find the right words."

"The right words for what? Just say it. You said it was about Warren."

"It is. Sort of." His dark eyes locked on mine. "He's…" he trailed off and sighed. "Listen, Sasha, I, I've been with Warren for a long time. He and I have been friends for five years now. Best friends. So, I need your utter confidence when I talk to you about this right now. I need to feel like I can trust you."

"Okay, what is it?"

Another sigh. "He has been with a lot of… all these years, it's been one basic girl after another. I'm telling you, women throw themselves at him. And, honestly, it's always the same kind of women." He paused and rubbed his own eyebrows again, sighing. "Listen, I'm not stupid. I know Warren's up there on a big stage with his guitar and his baseball cap and his blue eyes. I know what women see in him, and I know that I am the sidekick in this situation and not the star. I'm all right with that. Under normal circumstances, I'm just fine with it. I'm a confident person, and I don't need to try to compete with Warren.

He paused for several seconds, and I said, "Okay," since I didn't know where he was going with any of this.

"What I'm trying to say, Sasha, is that I am never discontent with the role I play in this relationship. I'm never jealous of Warren or his stuff. I support him and encourage him. That's why it works."

Jared stared at me. He was a handsome guy, and his stare was penetrating.

"But I can't take it with you. I'm sorry it's coming to this, but I don't think I can take him having someone like you. You're too real, and it's too much. I find that, that I want you."

He sounded sad, regretful, and I worked to figure out what in the world was going on. It felt like a trap.

"I always thought he would settle down with one of those basic, plastic girls that he's with all the time. I figured eventually he'd find one that stuck. That, I would've been fine with. But you're different. I would never expect him to end up with someone like you, Sasha. You're real, raw, natural, funny, thoughtful, beautiful. You're everything I want to end up with in life, and I can't see you and Warren—I love Warren, but I would be going crazy seeing you two together. It's torture. I mean, just watching you do that dance just now." He shook his head and sighed regretfully. "That's not like me to wish bad on Warren… we're boys."

"I'm sorry. I'm not trying to come between you guys," I said. "I would never want to do that."

Getting the words out was difficult. My mouth was dry and my lips stuck together when I spoke.

Jared stared straight at me, and I had no idea what to say or even think.

"We don't even have to say anything to him right now. We can just keep things like they are and get to know each other day by day. I need you to know that I'm interested in you though, Sasha. I'm interested in you for real, not like Warren. I want to develop a relationship with you. I would ask you to run away with me right now if I thought you were ready for that. Warren can have all the music, the women, the cars, and everything else in the world, but having you is just too much."

It was all so ridiculous and unbelievable that my first thought was that Warren had put his friend up to this as some kind of prank. I started to smile and joke about it, and then I realized that would be just as disturbing as if this whole thing were true.

My face was neutral. I was speechless, lost, and completely taken off-guard by the things he was saying. I had been making a conscious effort to impress Jared, but not because I liked him—it was because he was Warren's best friend. I was impressing him *for* Warren, on behalf of Warren.

"I would treat you like a queen, Sasha. I would move to Memphis with you and your brother, and I could make you happy."

I stared into his eyes, half expecting him to break into a smile and tell me this was a big joke. I waited there for what must've been twenty seconds, staring, thinking, feeling speechless.

I was completely taken aback when he leaned in.

In one swift movement, Jared kissed me.

His hand wrapped around the back of my head, and he kissed me with an imposing, open-mouthed kiss. His tongue was in my mouth for longer than a few heartbeats, and there was nothing I could do about it. He moaned when he pulled back, a pained moan like it was all he could do to stop himself from going any further.

"I'm sorry, I'm so sorry, Sasha," he said, instantly. He put his face in his hands and started to cry. I sat there and watched helplessly as this big guy hunched over and began bawling—his chest jumping and twitching as his breathing hitched. "I'm so sor-ry," he pleaded. "Please forgive me, Sasha."

I felt an odd sensation in my body—adrenaline, anxiety, or a mixture of the two—it was something I rarely experienced. I had a hot-cold sensation, like flashes of cold air were hitting my body.

"Please don't tell Warren," Jared said. He put his hand on my thigh with familiarity, and I pulled away. "Please, Sasha. I'm not going to do anything. I don't want to make you uncomfortable. That's the last thing I want."

I had been about to say that it was too late for that, but he stood up abruptly.

"I'm going to leave, Sasha, and I'm sorry. I’m really sorry to come in here like this. I hate it if you're mad at me right now."

I stared at him, at a complete loss for words.

"Please don't tell Warren we kissed," he said quietly.

We kissed.

We kissed.

The words wcrc abrasivc, likc sandpapcr.

I had no part in that. And somehow he was so pitiful and pained looking that I couldn’t get any words out to make my defense.

He started toward the door, and then he looked back. "I'm not going to say anything, and I'm not going to put you on the spot about it, but the offer is open, Sasha. My feelings are what they are."

He walked out, glancing at me with a sincere, regretful expression, and before I knew it, the door was closed behind him. *What had just happened to me?* My mouth was still raw and I had sensations on my skin where Jared had roughly kissed me. I wiped at the side of my mouth with the back of my hand.

Heartbeats passed, seconds passed. The seconds turned to minutes, and minutes passed. My mind was full and blank at the same time. I had been in the best mood of my life, and now I felt deflated, like balloon meets box cutter. I sat on the couch, staring at the wall in front of me and having no idea what to do or even think. I was revolted and disgusted. I felt like Jared had compromised my relationship with Warren, and that thought made me feel angry and violated.

I was up until after 4am having physical symptoms of anxiety. I went back and forth about telling Warren and not telling him, and I still had no idea what I was going to do. I was restless all night, and I woke up what must have been ten times.

Finally, I got a good chunk of sleep that lasted two hours. I woke up at 10am feeling thankful for a couple of uninterrupted hours. My stomach was still upset from what happened, though—I felt that right away. I looked at my phone, and my heart jumped when I saw that I had a text from Warren.

Warren:

Good morning honeybee! Call me when you get up.

It was in that moment that I decided to take the path of a strong-minded person. I had to mentally overcome this in order to keep my relationship with Warren intact, and there was just no way I was going to lose him over someone else's indiscretion. I had to be strong enough to deal with this, to get past it.

All night, I had replayed Jared's words, thinking about the women Warren had been with and all of the other seeds he had planted in my mind. It all hurt, but I knew I couldn’t let it destroy this thing I had going with Warren.

I had no idea whether or not I was going to tell him what Jared had done. It wasn't that I wanted to keep it from him. It was that I knew how much telling him would hurt him. It would change his life. If I kept it from him, it would only be for his own good.

If I told him, one of two things would happen. Either he would believe me and he would lose Jared, or something else would happen, and he would wind up losing me. I didn't want to think about that at the moment. I didn't want to tell Warren, I just wanted to see him.

Chapter 17

I texted Warren back.

Me:
I just woke up.

It was only a few seconds later when I heard back from him.

Warren:
Can I come see you?

Me:
Of course.

Warren:
Be there in 2min.

I liked his message and then I sprang out of bed like it was on fire. I flew into the bathroom and brushed my teeth before quickly washing my face and putting on a swipe of deodorant. I had barely finished with these incredibly quick tasks when I heard a knock on the door. I opened it, and there he was—jeans and a T-shirt. His hair was combed back and damp, and he had on no cap.

He stepped inside my room, and I walked straight into his arms.

"Are you okay?" he asked, gauging the style of my greeting.

"Yeah," I said, not even knowing it was a lie until it came out of my mouth. I held onto Warren, smelling him, feeling him, begging God to make a way for things to be okay with us.

"Show tonight," he said, having no idea what I was going through.

"I know," I replied.

Warren pulled back and smiled, taking in my face. He grinned and only hesitated in the entryway for a moment before moving. He kicked off his shoes, and took my hand, pulling me into the room.

"I thought we'd crash on your couch for a little while since it's still early," he said, walking that way.

But I just couldn't do it.

I couldn’t hold it in.

I had to get it off my chest.

The words, "Warren, I need to talk to you," came out before I could stop myself from saying them.

He instantly changed his expression to one of concern, and I gave him a regretful smile.

"What's the matter, bee?"

I had it all situated in my mind that I wasn't going to say anything because he had a show tonight, and everything went out the window when I was in his arms. I changed my mind again.

"I'm sorry," I said. "It's nothing. I just didn't sleep very well last night."

"Why not?" he asked, pulling me onto the couch with him. He sprawled out, hugging a pillow and then adjusting it, inviting me to go lie next to him. I took a few seconds to stretch out next to him. The couch was wide, and we hardly touched, we just laid there next to each other, on a mostly-horizontal plane rather than a vertical one.

"What's the matter?" he asked.

"I don't have any makeup on," I said.

"I'm not talking about that. I meant the look in your eyes."

I smiled, faking it, and then I closed my eyes and rolled toward him. "I'm just tired," I said.

I thought of how Jared kissed me. It flashed in my mind. It was so uncalled for.

"I think I might actually watch the concert from the stands tonight. I thought about finding an empty seat in the crowd, and that sounds fun… seeing you from the cheap seats."

"I'm fine with that, but you'd be more comfortable backstage with Jared. He'd take care of you."

I choked. I gagged on my own spit and coughed, sitting up, and pushing air out of my lungs to clear my throat.

"Sorry, (cough), I'm not… I-I'm good with watching the concert from upstage, upstairs, you know up by the normal… people… seats. Not backstage. I don't want to be backstage."

"Are you sure you're okay?"

"Yes, definitely," I said. "I just choked."

I gave my throat one last strategic clearing and then stretched out next to Warren again. The couch was roomy, and our bodies barely touched.

We stayed there and talked for the next two hours. I considered telling him about Jared what must've been twenty times, and every time, I decided it would be the selfish thing for me to do.

It was noon when I got up to use the restroom. Warren sat up and picked up his phone as I walked away.

"Hey, would you want to go grab some lunch with Jared and some of the band? Jared's texting, asking me about sushi."

"I'm… did you want to?"

"Yeah, I don't see why not. I usually eat a big meal for lunch on show days, and then ride it out on liquids and a protein bar until after the show."

"Yeah, I'm good with lunch," I said. "Whatever you want to do. I'm along for the ride… riding it out… seeing what happens. I'll need a little time to get dressed."

"Okay, I'm going back over to my room," he said. "Meet me over there when you're done—fifteen or twenty minutes? Thirty?"

"Twenty should be good," I said.

He stood up and stretched, and I could see his stomach when his t-shirt lifted up. He caught me looking, and he motioned with his hands for me to go back over there. I smiled and did it instantly, walking into his arms and hugging him, knowing this was goodbye for a minute.

Warren kissed me on the cheek, and I felt an electric zap of attraction, affection, and love. But then it quickly turned to something else, fear and maybe dread, when he pulled away and I remembered that there was a gigantic secret between us.

I had no idea whether or not I was doing the right thing. Keeping the secret and sharing it—both options were horrible.

"Jared was asking if you might want him to take you shopping or something before the show, while I'm busy at the venue."

"Shopping? For what? I don't care about shopping."

"Oh, I'm sorry. I wasn't saying you needed to… I just thought you might not want to be stuck at the venue all afternoon, and he offered."

"No, I'm the one who's sorry," I said. "That was really nice. But I'm not… I don't care for Jared as much as you do. I think I'm just going to chill by myself, if it's not the three of us. I might even stay back at the hotel."

I was nervous about saying those words, and my voice came out tentative and shaky even though I didn't mean for it to. Warren ducked, trying to get me to look at him.

"Did something happen?" he asked.

And the words caused a flash of the memory of Jared's imposing kiss, and I cringed.

"Sasha."

"I'm sorry. I'm just saying that the only time I want to be around Jared is if it's the three of us. I don't get along with him when we're by ourselves."

"When were you by yourselves?" he asked, looking curious.

"Was Jared drinking last night?" I asked. "Does he ever do drugs or anything else that makes him act weird?"

"No. Why? Did he say something to you?"

I could tell he was completely confused. This was coming out of nowhere for him. We had told each other goodnight and there had been no beef between Jared and me at that point.

"I really want you to just play your gig for the next two nights. I don't want you to think about me or what I'll be doing because you already have enough on your plate. I'm just telling you right now that I'm going to be avoiding Jared. I don't like him."

"Would you mind explaining?" he asked tilting his head and looking at me with a sweet, patient expression.

"I don't know. Do you trust him?"

"I did, until about twenty seconds ago."

"No, no, I'm sorry. I was wondering if he's ever given you a reason to, you know, not trust him."

"No, he hasn't. He makes good money at his job, and I pay for his room and food when he travels with me. Are you talking about stealing my stuff or stealing from me? Did you see something?"

He sounded so confused like he absolutely couldn't believe Jared would ever have any charges brought against him.

I swallowed hard, trying to decide in those crucial seconds how much I wanted to tell him.

"Jared came on to me last night."

Warren looked concerned for a second but then his face broke into a smile. "Oh no, he's just teasing you, bee, are you talking about how he was messing with you last night? He's like that with everybody."

"No, Warren. He came in my room last night."

Warren instantly stiffened and pulled back, looking at me with a serious expression, gauging whether or not I was joking. He continued to focus on my face.

"He what?"

"I didn't want to tell you any of this because I want tonight and the rest of this tour to go smoothly. I want the rest of your life to go smoothly."

"Jared came into your room?" he asked, squinting at me.

"Yes. Last night. He texted me and said he needed to talk, so I let him in, and then… Warren…"

"What happened?"

"He just told me a bunch of stuff about liking me."

"He is sappy sometimes," Warren said.

"It wasn't sappiness," I said. "It was more than that, and it made me uncomfortable enough that I just don't want to be alone with him. I already thought about all of this, and I don't want to mess up your friendship, or your concert tonight, or anything else. I'm not trying to have a big fight, and I don't need you to confront Jared, but I'm also not okay with being alone with him—pretty much ever again."

"Did he touch you?" Warren asked.

The question was unexpected.

"What do you mean?" I asked.

"Did he touch you?" he said it slower. "Did he lay a hand on you?"

The kiss.

The unwanted, unsolicited kiss.

A vision of it flashed in my mind.

It was one-sided, and it was not okay for him to do it.

"Yes."

"Yes?"

"Yes," I said.

"Yes, he touched you?"

"Yes."

"What do you mean by that?" he asked, trying to maintain his composure. "Please elaborate, Sasha."

I let out the breath I had been holding. "He kissed me."

"A peck?"

"No."

Warren turned around putting his face in his hands. "Please tell me you're lying."

"I wish I was."

He was quiet for a few seconds. "Did you take part in this?" he asked numbly.

"No. Goodness. No, Warren. Of course not. I don't even want to ever see him again. I was thinking about just catching an early flight back to Memphis."

"Sasha, no. You have to tell me what happened. He's a hugger. Are you sure he meant it like that kind of kiss?"

"Warren, I wish I was overreacting. I wish I was making this out to be more than it was. But he told me that he wanted me—that he was jealous of you having me, and then he kissed me. It was not a kiss like you kiss a friend."

"I am so sorry, Sasha. What time was this?"

"It was after you came in my room. The only thing I could think of was drugs, but you said he wasn't on any drugs."

"Did he seem like he was on drugs? Was he acting like that?"

"No. Other than trying to push himself on me."

He stared down at the floor.

"What are you thinking?" I asked.

"He has never done anything like this before. I just talked to him this morning. I trust him with everything. He has keys to my house in his pocket."

"I'm so sorry," I said. "I feel like I should just go back to Memphis. I don't want you to have to deal with this while you're out on tour."

"I just want to make sure that I know exactly what happened before I go take care of it. I need you to confirm that he was being inappropriate."

"He was being inappropriate, but I understand if you—"

I stopped talking mid-sentence because Warren turned and began walking away, heading for the door.

"Are you leaving?"

"I'm going to take care of it," he said, glancing back at me with a serious expression.

I started to move, and he put a hand out to stop me.

"Stay in here," he said. "I'm going in there alone. I'll come back in here after I take care of this. It might be a while, though. Just stay in here. You can get room service. Or you can obviously leave the hotel if you need to. Just give me some time in the room with Jared. Don't come over to that room, please."

"I'm sorry, Warren."

"I'm the one who's sorry," he said. I could tell, simply from the expression on his face, that he had resolved to deal with Jared.

Chapter 18

Warren Manning

Warren was fuming. He was red-hot with anger as he walked down the hallway toward his own hotel room. This was the absolute last thing he imagined having to deal with today. He loved and trusted Jared, and yet somehow he knew Sasha was telling the truth and Jared was at fault.

He knew Jared liked Sasha, but he never dreamed he would try anything like this. It was a type of betrayal that blindsided Warren. It had him experiencing physical symptoms. His chest felt like it wanted to explode. His palms were sweaty, and he sensed that there was an eminent physical exchange between the two gentlemen.

Warren's teeth were clenched as he opened the door. Jared was sitting in the kitchen. He had his laptop out, but he was looking Warren's way by the time Warren noticed him there.

"Hey, what's up? Are we all going to lunch? I promised the boys." Jared said nonchalantly.

It was with great difficulty that Warren worked to maintain his composure. He walked across the suite, toward the kitchen area where Jared was sitting. Jared stared at Warren curiously, waiting for the answer to his question.

"Sasha didn't want to go to lunch with you," Warren said. He was only a few feet away from Jared by now, staring at the way Jared reacted.

He was surprised and confused. "Is she sick or something?"

"No, Jared, she's not sick." Warren's eyes locked with Jared's. Jared smiled a little, and Warren's serious expression held.

"What's up, brother?" Jared said, looking a little more concerned.

Warren nudged his head. "You know what's up."

Jared put his hands in the air and leaned back in his chair casually. "I'm afraid I don't. You're going to have to tell me."

"Did you kiss her?"

"Whoa, whoa, what? Who?"

"Jared. Did you?"

"Sasha?"

"Yes."

"Look, I texted her last night and went over there to try to get a surprise together *for you*."

"You tried to get a surprise together for me?" Warren asked, squinting at his best friend.

"Yes. You can read my texts. It was about you. I went over there to ask her about that gig in Miami. I knew you wanted her to stay longer than two days, so I was trying to work that out for you."

"So, you went over there as a favor to me, and then nothing happened? You didn't try to kiss her?"

"Yes, oh, yes, I tried to kiss your girlfriend," Jared said the words sarcastically. "Did she actually try to accuse me of that?"

"Jared. Tell me the truth."

"Bro. No offense, Sasha's great and everything, but you saw Lindsey." (Jared was referring to the woman he brought back to the suite with him when they were in Panama.) "I'm actually talking to her right now."

"Sasha?"

"Lindsey," Jared said. "She might come to the Miami show."

Jared was a good liar. Warren would have believed him if he didn't believe and love Sasha.

In those seconds, Warren decided he would have to become an even better liar than his friend.

"Jared, I thought you were my boy. I can't understand how you would lie to my face like this."

"What?" He laughed. "What are you talking about?"

"Jared, cut it out. Sasha had her laptop there, and the camera caught you."

"Then you could see that nothing happened," Jared said. But he was agitated and he began sweating instantly. He stood up, shifting restlessly.

"I know what happened, Jared." Warren spoke with such conviction it was as if he had seen the fake video evidence.

Jared stepped back like he was going to start to walk away, and then suddenly, he reared back and blindsided Warren with a right hand to the face. Jared held nothing back with the force applied during that first punch, and a fight ensued.

Warren tackled his friend to the floor and they rolled, banging into the side of a couch. Time seemed to stand still as Warren postured up and struck Jared in the jaw. He punched Jared, and Jared kicked and flailed, swinging and missing Warren completely.

Jared stood up, and Warren stepped back cautiously. But then Jared swung at him again—a right hook. Warren ducked, causing what would have been a crushing blow to barely hit him. Warren had a good shot at Jared's side, and he took it, causing Jared to moan and lean over.

There was a scramble. Jared was desperate, and he swung hard and fast, but Warren had his wits about him, and he weathered the storm before a couple of final blows that left Jared on the floor waving him off. He sputtered a stream of obscenities and then made a statement about how messed up it was to let a woman get in the way of a friendship.

There was blood. Warren's face was throbbing where he had been punched, and there was blood dripping down the side of Jared's jaw where his lip was cut. Several blows had been exchanged. Warren had a rough childhood, and he had been in more than a few fights. Jared was a big guy, but he was no match for Warren, who not only had experience fighting but also really loved Sasha and wanted to protect her.

Jared could see he stood no chance, and he retreated, stepping back and holding up his hand and a gesture that made it obvious he was giving up. He cussed some more, yelling at Warren. There had been a fistfight between the two men, and unbelievably, Warren had not been the one to start it. Jared kept shouting accusations and obscenities as he gathered his things.

Warren watched it all with a numb, distant feeling. He marveled at the fact that he completely trusted Jared. Warren prided himself on being able to judge people's character, and this had come so out of left field that Warren just sat there, feeling stunned and not knowing what to do.

They had a few exchanges where Jared stated the fact that he was going back to Nashville to get his things from Warren's house. There was a motorcycle that Warren had paid for but they always considered to be Jared's, and Jared had the nerve to tell Warren that he was taking the motorcycle. Warren was so blindsided by the whole thing that he couldn't take in how weird it was for Jared to do that. There was a lot of shouting as Jared gathered his things and left. There were accusations and defenses, but Warren tuned all of them out as he sat there evaluating the whole situation and feeling the sting from the blow to his face.

His body was throbbing in two or three different places, but the area on his face was the worst. His cheek was sore and there was a cut near his eyebrow. Warren closed his eyes and sighed at the memory of it happening.

Warren just sat there and prayed for patience while Jared packed his things. He didn't care about Jared finding a way home or what he did once he got there. He didn't care about the motorcycle. He sent a text to Becky letting her know that he and Jared were no longer on speaking terms and for her to please put any of his things, along with the blue motorcycle, out front for him to pick up. He made sure she knew to include the Triumph and not his blue Bishop. He added that he wanted all of his locks changed.

Becky didn't ask for an explanation. They had a short conversation via text during the time when Jared packed and yelled and yelled and packed. It took him fifteen minutes or so to get his things and get out of the suite, and Warren didn't get off the couch until the door was closed and locked behind him. He texted Becky again, saying he needed his suite keys changed, and within minutes, the concierge brought up new keycards for his room.

"Is everything okay?" The concierge was normally extremely professional but his face broke into a worried grimace when he noticed Warren's face.

"I'm fine," Warren said touching his own cheek. He knew there was blood there. He could feel it on his fingers. "I'm fine," he added, sounding resolute.

The concierge, being the professional he was, nodded and told Warren to call if he needed anything else. The man was used to that rockstar stuff, anyway. There had been fights in rooms before. Warren wasn't the first bad-boy musician type to stay here and he wouldn't be the last.

His concerned reaction did, however, prompt Warren to take a shower before going next door to see Sasha. He spent more time than usual in the shower, letting the water run over him and thinking about the sequence of events. His room would no doubt feel empty when he got out of the shower. It already felt empty. Warren's band was there, four guys who traveled with him and stayed in the same hotel. He got along well with them, but Warren was a solo act and they were hired hands. Warren would have their company after Sasha went back to Memphis, but he was used to traveling with Jared, and his life would inevitably seem a little quiet and empty.

In those moments, as the water hit him in the shower, he felt the weight of Jared's betrayal. He felt the weight of impending loneliness. He replayed, in his mind, the moment when Jared realized he had been caught. His immediate reaction had been to fight—to strike Warren.

Warren had held his ground, but that first punch was a complete surprise, and his temple ached where it had happened. Several places on his body had been hit in the exchange. His back and his leg had places that ached.

He was sure Jared got the worst of it, though. The moment had passed in such a blur of passion, but he knew he had gotten the best of Jared. *How had it come to this? How had this happened?* Warren had finally found the woman who could make him happy, and he had to trade in his best friend in the process.

Maybe it was better this way. Maybe things would've been even worse if the process had been slower and more drawn out. If Jared was willing to commit this type of betrayal, Warren wondered what else he was capable of.

But maybe it was just a matter of love. Maybe Jared was a trustworthy person in general, Sasha was just too strong of a temptation for him to resist. Maybe Sasha was so special that no one could resist her.

Those thoughts made Warren feel more protective of her than ever. He thought of Jared going over to her room and making advances on her. He thought of how sweet she had been this morning, trying not to tell him. She seemed timid, and the memory of it lit a fire within Warren.

He turned off the shower and went to the task of drying off and getting dressed. He would go to Sasha and he would protect her. He would make things right. He had been the one who put her in the situation with Jared, and it was up to him to make sure she was protected in the future.

Warren remembered the Jesus sign on the road on the way to see her, and it made him stop and pray that he could do a better job of protecting her in the future. He was devastated by the morning's events, and he obviously wished none of it had happened, but he still believed he was on the right path.

Chapter 19

Sasha Faulkner

Warren was gone for over an hour, and it seemed like an absolute eternity. I had no idea what was going on next door. It was possible that Warren was peaceably taking care of the whole thing. They could have a decent conversation where Jared would admit to everything and he would leave, never to be heard from again.

But I knew in my heart that was an unlikely scenario. Jared could have been making up horrible lies about me. Maybe Warren believed it all, and I would never hear from him again. I went through moments in my thoughts when I half expected the hotel staff to come in and kick me out. I had a knot in my stomach and a feeling that was a surreal mix of hope and dread. I was sort of floating in a state of confused paranoid hope while he was gone. I had no idea what to expect or when to expect it.

I spent some time getting dressed and making myself presentable to go out because I figured that was the logical thing to do no matter what happened.

I went to the door when I finally heard knocking. I glanced through the peephole and saw Warren standing there.

The relief was instant and it manifested as a whooshing sensation that I felt physically when I opened the door. I pulled him inside and threw myself into his arms. He was eager to end up in that same position, and he took me into his embrace. Thank goodness.

He smelled clean and his skin had that still-damp texture like he had just gotten out of the shower. I was so happy to hug him and have him hug me that I hardly looked at his face. After a few seconds, I pulled back to focus on him.

"You look beautiful," he said, focusing on me at the same time.

But I didn't have my wits about me enough to thank him for the compliment because I was too busy noticing the cut on his face. It was a small gash at the top of his cheek, near the corner of his eye. There was other redness and some swelling. I reached up for it, and he pulled away.

"It's fine," he said when our eyes met.

I blinked, tears coming to my eyes when I realized he had been hurt. "What happened?"

He shrugged. "I told him I knew, and we had an exchange about it." We were quiet for a few seconds before he continued. "He's gone. He left."

"Where did he go?"

Warren shrugged. "Back to Nashville. I don't know. He might move since he works remote. I really don't know what he'll do. It's crazy to say that."

"Is he gone for good?"

"Yes."

"I'm sorry," I said.

"Don't, Sasha. Please don't say that. I'm the one who's sorry." He squeezed my hand. "You look like you're ready to go."

"I was kind of ready for anything," I said with a little shrug.

"Let's go get lunch," he said. "It'll be good for both of us to get out of here for a minute—talk about everything somewhere other than in this hotel room."

"That sounds amazing," I said. "Can I see your thing before we go?"

I gestured to his cut, but he didn't see me and he said, "What thing?"

"Your face."

Warren turned and tilted his head so that I could get a look at the cut.

"I guess it's not deep enough to need stitches."

"Na," he said.

"It's a little swollen," I added, inspecting it.

"I know. It's fine, though. It'll go down. It's not the worst I've had."

"It's not the worst punch to the face you've ever had?"

"No. You know that about me. You know how I grew up. I knew something was off with him last night. I could feel it. I didn't know what it was, but I felt something." He let out a big sigh. "Let's talk about it later."

It was easy to see that he didn't feel like elaborating much on Jared right then, and I certainly didn't want to push him to do so.

It was only a minute later when Warren and I left my room, heading to lunch. He stayed right beside me, opening doors and maintaining a general posture of protecting me and caring for me. He barely touched my back when I walked through doors, and he didn't hold my hand or make any other contact with me.

We were walking next to each other when we saw two members of the band in the lobby. Thomas and Alex sat on a couch in one of the seating areas, and Warren waved at them. I hadn't met them before but Warren filled me in right when he noticed them.

"That's Thomas and Alex on the green couch. Do you mind if they come to lunch?" He asked the question before we walked over there.

"Not at all," I agreed quietly.

"What's up?" said the one with curly hair. "Who's this and where's Jared, he's buying us lunch, but he's not texting me back. He said we might go to sushi."

"Oh, then I'm buying you lunch because Jared's not coming. And this is Sasha."

"Hey, oh, yeah, Sasha, we've heard about you. I knew you were coming to Florida, but I didn't realize it was Tampa. It's nice to meet you. I'm Thomas. Where's Jared?"

"He went back to Nashville," Warren said. "I don't talk about Jared anymore."

"Is that what your face is about?" Alex, the quieter one asked.

"I wasn't going to say anything," Thomas said.

They both stood up.

"Yes, the cut is from Jared, and yes, he looked worse. I also should mention that if he comes back around, to the hotel, or backstage, or anywhere else, he's not welcome."

"Whoa, heavy."

"Yes, heavy. But it's over, and it's fine. I'm good, and I don't want to talk about it anymore."

"Ten-four," Thomas said with a nod.

"I'm buying lunch. Where do you guys want to go?"

"We talked about sushi, but I'd rather Mexican," Thomas said. "There's a place down the street with good reviews, and I'm starving."

The four of us took off walking down the street.

Thomas was outgoing and Alex was quiet, but they both possessed quick wit and a dry sense of humor. It was interesting to watch Warren grow more and more relaxed as our lunch went on.

He had been hit in the face. There was a cut near his eye and a red mark around the cut, extending down to his cheek. There was slight swelling, but I tried not to stare at it. Looks-wise, it only added to his bad-boy appeal.

I just hoped things could get back on track with us. I knew he wasn't upset with me, but I still had questions, and there was a general sense of not being fully settled. Maybe I just felt that way because he still wasn't holding my hand.

We went through all of lunch with the guys with no physical contact. Warren continued to care for me, but there was no touching. I hated it. I longed for him to touch me—even a brush of his hand on mine would have been such a relief.

We had a good time at lunch, though, and I did experience an overall feeling of relief that Warren was smiling and sitting there with me. I knew he believed me instead of Jared, and I knew they had parted ways because of it. That was all I needed for now.

We discussed all sorts of things while we ate with Alex and Thomas. They were funny and had a cool, laidback band dynamic. It was easy to fall into rhythm with them, and I did fine with it in spite of feeling a little distracted by yearning for Warren's touch.

We talked and laughed together as we walked back to the hotel. It was in the lobby where we ran into the final two members of his band. Dawson and Lane. I had the knack for recognizing band members now, and I knew who they were before we even walked up to them.

We talked for ten or fifteen minutes in the lobby, and the guys decided to go out again while Warren and I opted for heading upstairs. They had plans to meet again in a few hours when they left for the venue. Warren and I said goodbye to them, and then headed through the hotel lobby, walking toward the elevator. We got inside and smiled at each other.

A woman slipped into the elevator just before the door closed. She giggled and stood in the corner, smiling at Warren who was waiting for her to say what floor she needed. The door closed and the elevator started to move during her hesitation.

"I'm so sorry, I'm not actually… going up," she said in a breathless, nervous voice that had me feeling wary of her. I pulled back staring at her and she put her hands up in surrender. "I'm just… I just saw that it was you, Warren Manning, and I had to jump in the elevator. My family is downstairs waiting for me, and I'll ride down after you get off. I'm sorry if it's weird. I'm not weird. Strange, I mean. I am weird, but I'm not strange. Dangerous. I'm just a fan. I've been loving your music since your first single, and I listen to every single album on repeat, so I know all the words by heart and everything. I'm sorry. You are Warren Manning, aren't you? Of course you are. I'm sorry about all this. I usually don't trap myself in small boxes with people, but I just saw you, and my body reacted before I had the chance to think about how odd this was. Oh, you're stopping on the seventh floor. I didn't mean to see what floor you were on."

I actually felt bad for the girl. She was young, and obviously starstruck by seeing Warren. She felt bad for babbling, and she just couldn't make herself stop.

"We're not actually on…" Warren started to speak, but a woman from the housekeeping staff walked into the elevator, pushing a cart.

"Going up?" she asked, causing Warren and me to nod. She got onto the elevator with her cart and then reached out to push the button for the tenth floor.

"Is it horrible for me to ask for a picture?" the woman asked, staring at him from across the cart.

"No, it's not," he said. The elevator dinged and I looked up to find that we were already on the tenth floor. The housekeeper got off of the elevator, apologizing for the interruption, and the door closed again.

Warren stepped to the side while the girl used her phone to take a selfie of the two of them. I watched as she stood next to Warren and snapped a photo. He had lots of practice at these, and he smiled like he was a professional, conveniently turning to the side so that his cut wasn't visible in the photo.

The girl shook like a leaf the whole time. He asked her name, and she said it was Erin. He told her it had been nice meeting her, and just like that, we got off of the elevator on our own floor. Erin stayed inside the elevator as the door closed.

Warren's room was huge and quiet, and we went into it. "Do you want to hang out on the couch and watch some TV he asked?"

"I'm leaving you alone so you can get in the zone before your show."

He smiled at me. "You are my zone. I still have another hour, at least, before I need to get ready."

So, we kicked off our shoes and sat on the couch together. At first, we talked about surface-level things, but then we got into a conversation about Jared, and he elaborated on everything that transpired earlier.

I was there, sitting on his couch, for over an hour, and it seemed like only a few seconds. I leaned forward and peered at the clock on the wall, gasping when I realized what time it was.

"I need to let you do your thing," I said, standing. "Do you mind if I get another bottled water out of your fridge before I go back?"

"No," he said. "Take whatever you want out of there."

Warren had a stocked fridge, and I took a bottled water and a bottle of juice—some kind of cranberry cocktail drink. I set the bottle of water down and then I opened and took a sip of the cranberry juice. I looked into the living room after I twisted the top back into position.

Warren was staring at me. He wasn't smiling but he also wasn't scowling—his expression was neutral, and the lightness of his eyes was piercing, even from across the room. He was kicked back with his arms resting along the back and side of the couch. He adjusted, sitting up and repositioning his arms. His gaze stayed locked on me the entire time. He was unbelievably handsome. I was attracted to him on a physical level, and I also loved him.

It hurt that he hadn't touched me at all today. I longed for him. I felt a yearning sensation that made it difficult to stay in the kitchen, this far away from him. We had been together for hours, and not once that whole time had he taken me into his arms.

I stared at him, feeling desperate to be near him even though I had technically just left his side. We had been having a great time together, and somehow it felt like I hadn't been with him all day.

"What are you thinking?" he asked.

I shrugged and smiled, buying myself a second to think of a response. "I was thinking about you," I said.

"What about me?" he asked.

"That I like you."

"I'm thinking I like you, too," he said, smiling a little.

My lower abdomen was in knots, and I felt like I was on the edge of some kind of precipice. It took all of my strength to stay in place and not cross the room and collapse into his arms.

"I’m waiting on you, you know." His words were soft and sweet, and I was so swept away by his gaze that I hardly took them in.

"What?"

"I'm waiting on you," he repeated. "I'm giving you space after last night. I don't want to rush you into letting me be near you, physically."

"Oh, m-me? Yeah, no, I, uh, I wasn't thinking I needed any… space."

Warren got to the edge of the couch, sitting up, staring at me like he was at a starting line.

My heart raced and I stared at him, knowing he wanted to come to me. "I was worried maybe you weren't attracted to me after what happened with Jared," I said.

"You thought I wasn't attracted to you?"

"Yes, that's what I was thinking. I couldn't think of any other reason why you wouldn't want to…"

"Because I was giving you time," he said. "I assumed you wouldn't want me to try to touch you for a while after what he did."

"That was sweet, but…"

"But what?"

"But I would have been fine with it." I put my hands on the bottles as if about to pick them up. "I don't need any space or time, if that's what you were thinking."

Warren sprang off of the couch and took four or five leaping bounds toward me, causing me to let out a little laugh. By the time I turned around, he had covered the remaining distance and was advancing on me. He didn't stop moving until right on top of me, staring down at me from only inches away.

Chapter 20

I was gloriously trapped between the kitchen counter and my man, staring at his face, into his blue eyes from only inches away. I had just told him that I didn't need time to get over what Jared did to me, and it took him all of two seconds to make his way over to me.

I took an uneven breath, taking tiny gasps inward. He used his fingertip and touched the side of my face. His gaze was scorching. "Do you promise you're okay?" he asked sweetly.

"I'm so much better now," I said breathlessly.

I stretched upward and placed a quick kiss on the underside of his jaw. He instantly let out the breath he had been holding, causing his chest to fall.

He pulled me closer as he breathed, leaning down where his mouth was almost touching mine. I shifted, getting my lips even closer to his. I could feel the warmth of his breath on my mouth. I had been aching for him so badly that my body pulsed and tingled with sensations that were new and foreign.

"I missed you," I said weakly.

"Sasha, I love you, and I missed you too. I've just been trying to create this invisible forcefield around you all day—to protect you from everyone. Including myself."

"I don't need to be protected from you," I said, whispering.

"I want you to please try to find a way to stay with me."

"When do you mean? Right now?"

"No, although you can stay in this room as much as you want. I would let you move in if you wanted to. I was talking about being with you for good. I need to get you closer to Nashville. In Nashville. With me. In my house." His mouth was so near mine that his lips brushed against mine when he spoke. "Can you be with me more, please?"

I thought of school for a split second, and I quickly realized it didn't matter. "Yes," I said, not caring what he meant. I closed the half-inch that separated our mouths, leaning upward to let my lips press against his. Warren let me drive the kiss. He was gentle and caring, and I knew he let me set the pace as a gesture of kindness. I reached up and held onto his face, holding him steady, kissing him gently again and again. My gut ached because he met my kiss with the perfect reception—he was gentle with me and he kissed me back. His lips were soft and warm, and I had been aching to touch him for hours. The amount of relief was so great, I felt like I could cry. I had been overthinking the reasons he would create distance, and it was like I could finally breathe now that I realized he wanted me.

Our light connection slowly, gradually moved into something more urgent. I opened my mouth to him, and he kissed me deeply. We were skin to skin, mouth to mouth, body to body. Warren held me there, kissing me and assuring me that he wanted me. There was no mistaking that he wanted me. His body was rigid and lined with muscles, and he held me in place against the counter. My eyes were full of tears when he finally pulled back.

"Are we good?" he said. "Do we need to talk about the Jared thing more? Are you okay?"

"I'm one hundred percent okay," I said. "I can't believe you got in a fight, and I'm sorry about your eye, but I'm fine if you are. Do you think he's going to come back? You know, asking your forgiveness?"

"I don't know, this has never happened before. I can't imagine he would."

"Are you okay about everything?"

"Yes. I'm upset that it happened, but this is the only reasonable outcome, considering the situation."

"Thank you for everything today. Thank you for this, thank you for this moment."

I knew I needed to leave, so I turned to get the drink bottles. Warren held me in place from behind. He leaned down, placing his mouth near my neck. "I love you," he said. "And I'm going to see you in a minute. Just come back over here and let yourself in when you're done getting ready."

He took hold of me, steadying me as he leaned with me in his arm. He moaned, reaching, stretching. I laughed when I realized what he was doing. There were room keys on his counter, and he stretched out and retrieved one, handing it to me. I started to take it, but he held it up, out of my grasp, like I owed him something for it.

"What are you asking me for?" I asked, not moving.

Warren nudged his chin at me. It was a small movement, but I knew he was asking for a kiss.

"Oh, you'll give it to me for a kiss? Because I want to kiss you, anyway. I kissed him, and in the same motion, he handed me the key. I loved his mouth. I could not believe he was about to open that mouth and sing to thousands of people.

"I'll be back in a little bit," I said. "I'll text before I walk over here."

***

Three of the guys from the band were in Warren's suite by the time I made my way back over there. He looked regretful about their presence when he met me at the door, but I assured him that I didn't mind. It took a lot of work to communicate with and organize five guys into a band dynamic. They were all good people who had been with Warren for a while, and it was neat for me to see the way they interacted before the show.

I did my best to stay out of their way, and just like that, we were leaving. I sat next to him in the van on the way there, but we weren't preoccupied with each other. It was hectic and loud, and they all interacted so much that I mostly stayed quiet. I didn't mind at all. It was interesting to see the way they got hyped. I was familiar with a backstage routine with theater, but things were different with a band.

They had a greenroom at the venue where everyone hung out until it was time for the show. This one was in a large room (that wasn't green) backstage. It was more relaxed than a theater setting where we were all hustling around the dressing rooms.

We had a few hours to kill backstage while waiting for him to go on. There was soundcheck and an opening band, a local group. Their music was loud, even from the green room.

It was mostly guys back there with us. There were a few employees of the venue who were in and out, and a couple of them were women, but I hadn't talked to any of them. I had been keeping to myself when Warren was busy. I was normally a talkative, friendly person, but I was understandably skittish about getting too close to his friends after everything with Jared.

Warren was standing on the other side of the room, talking to two of the band members when a woman walked up to me.

"Are you here with Warren?" she asked. She was older than me, but not by much… I couldn't tell exactly. She was pretty, though, and I smiled at her, feeling surprised that she came over and addressed me directly.

"Me, yes. I am here with Warren. Is it okay?"

"Yeah, oh, of course. I'm… Warren's one of my favorites in the world. What's your name?"

"Sasha."

"Well, I have a good spot out there in the front—a space reserved at the rail. I can't believe he's playing here. I didn't know if you wanted to come out there with me. We could dance."

There was music from the opening band, and she started moving to demonstrate. The two of us grinned at each other.

"I didn't really have a plan," I said. "I was just going to watch from backstage."

"Oh, do you not want to go into the audience?" she asked. "Because you can't get a better spot than mine."

I stood up, straightening my clothes and looking at her. She was all dressed up in jeans and a sequin top with boots. She was beautiful, and she smiled at me with an inviting smile. I thought going to the audience with her would be fun. Just then, I turned and noticed Warren walking up to us. He put his hand on my back.

"Hey, I'm going on stage in a second to sit in on a song with this band. I'll be back again before my set."

I nodded and Warren gestured in such a way that invited me to kiss him. I leaned that way, and he kissed me. His mouth landed near mine.

"I'll be back in a minute," he said.

I nodded. "Do you mind if I go watch the show with… what's your name?"

"Jesse. I've already told Warren what a big fan I am. Look, I've been working here for five years, and rarely do I take the night off and watch a concert from the pit. Come on, let me party with your girlfriend. We'll be down there dancin'—right where you can keep your eyes on us."

"Do you want to go?" he asked, looking at me.

Jesse was a forward type person and she roped her arm in mine. "Sure, she does."

"Warren!" someone called for him from the door and he gave me a regretful parting glance.

"I'll be fine," I said.

"She'll be fine. I'll bring her back here after the show," Jesse assured him.

"Oh, my gosh, girl, he's protective of you," she said to me when he walked away. "I don't know what I'd give to have Warren Manning look at me like that. No offense, I mean, I'm not trying to steal your man, I'm just saying, you're one lucky woman. What happened to his face? Was it a bar fight? I'm so sorry, but he's hot. Your boyfriend is fire." She spoke quickly as she pulled me along, going toward the door. "I'm trying to get you out there in time to see this song," she explained. "Do you need to grab anything?"

"No, I'm good."

I had a small bag situated across my body. It contained my wallet, phone, keys, and some lip gloss. It was all I brought with me.

Jesse took me by the hand and pulled me with her. She knew the venue like the back of her hand and we weaved through doorways and groups of people like it was nothing. We approached the crowd from the side and made our way to the foot of the stage, weaving through people.

"What's up, Kevin?" she said when we got close to the guard who was standing there with his back toward the stage.

"What's up, Jesse? Are you coming to watch already?"

"Just this next song," she said. "Warren's coming out to sing."

Kevin made a face like he was dreading the repercussions of Warren coming onto the stage. He made room for us at the rail, showing the women beside us that there was tape reserving our place. They pushed and shoved to get in next to us.

I spent the next ten minutes in wonder as I watched Warren get introduced by the opening band and come on stage. He interacted with the other band, and then they performed a song together. I had heard them go over it earlier, so I knew the song they would sing, and I still felt surprised and overwhelmed by the whole experience.

The people around me, including Jesse, all knew the lyrics to the song, and they sang along. I could have caught on by the end of it, but I opted to just stand there and take it all in. The crowd begged him to stay up there for one more song, and they played a fast one that had everyone dancing.

Jesse and I danced. I thought of Warren up there singing, and I wondered what he was thinking, but I figured he was doing his thing, and I got lost in the music, dancing, doing my own thing.

Before I knew it, the song was ending and the lead singer of the band said, "Warren Manning, everyone!"

The crowd exploded with cheers as Warren stood from his stool, waving. He gave me a wink before he left the stage.

Jesse turned to me. "Did you see him wink at you?"

"Yes," I said, smiling at her.

"We have about thirty minutes before he goes back on with his band," she said. "I have to go restock some things at the bar. You can stay here with Kevin and hold our spot, or I'll walk you back to the green room."

"I guess I'll go to the green room," I said.

Jesse took my hand, and again we walked smoothly and sharply through all the people, heading to the back. It was a type of chaos that I was not accustomed to but Jesse was right at home there, and she pulled me along, talking to people and checking in with them as we walked.

"I assume you want to come and watch the show with me now that you've seen my spot," she said, glancing back at me and smiling.

"Yeah, I think so," I agreed.

We walked through the backstage door with no problems or questions from the guys who were guarding it. They had seen us come out, and they knew Jesse, so they just gave us a wave and let us open the door.

"I'll come back and get you right before they go on," she said.

"Thank you, Jesse."

She looked at me with a smile. "Thank you," she said. "We're going to have fun. I'm pumped that I get to stand next to Warren's… there he is now. I was just telling your lady that I'm happy to have her with me. We're going to have fun tonight. Girls' night."

Warren smiled at Jesse as he reached out for me. His smile was so handsome and irresistible that my chest ached.

"Thank you," he said to her.

He pulled me down the hall, and we went into a room together. It was the first door on the right, and it was marked 'employees only'. I thought it was a broom closet or office, but it was too dark to tell. Warren pulled me inside and locked the door behind us. He leaned against the backside of the door, pulling me into his arms. The door clicked, and there was no light in the room with us whatsoever. I giggled at how unexpected the whole thing was. It was dark, and my eyes still struggled to adjust.

"I'm sorry, I don't know where the light switch is and I don't really care. I just wanted to get you in here for a minute and tell you that I… I saw you dancing down there, and you're just the most adorable thing I've ever seen. That night we met, you told me that music heals. I think I fell in love with you at that very moment. I've honestly never looked at other women the same way after that. I saw you in the audience just now, and I remembered you saying that to me. I just love you, and I need you. I want you to try to come be near me in Nashville."

"I love you, too, and yes to Nashville or whatever you have in mind," I said, feeling shy and at a loss for words.

He leaned down and kissed me. A brief but deep kiss, like a possessive stamp that had me reeling. I felt melted when he pulled away.

"Okay, let's go, I have a concert to play."

Warren opened the door and stepped into the hallway, his hand in mine.

Epilogue

Nine months later
Mid-Summer
Nashville

My brother, August, was currently in Nashville, staying with Warren and me. He had just gotten here yesterday, and he had plans to stay with me for the weekend while Warren went out of town for work. It had been almost a month since Warren and I got married, and we had been traveling since then, so I hadn't seen August in a while. It was nice to have him over.

I had just moved to Nashville in May, after I finished college. The wedding and honeymoon had dominated most of my life since then, and the whole summer felt like a blur. We had been back in Nashville for a little over a week, and everything still felt new to me.

Since we'd been home, we adopted the most gorgeous little golden retriever puppy. We named him Buddy on account of Warren always fantasizing about having a dog with that name. He long since had the resources to get a puppy, but he never felt settled enough to do it. Warren had told me countless times that he was relieved to find the person he was going to build a life with.

We didn’t make any specific plans, but we both wanted a good home life with a family eventually. Warren liked to say what a good mom I was going to be, and he talked about what a big bunch of kids we were going to have eventually. I had always wanted a family, and I was happy that he wanted to start one at some point. He had a rough time growing up, and he was determined to forge a different path for his own children.

But for now, Warren was busy with his career, and this marriage and moving to Nashville was all still so new. Adopting Buddy seemed like a logical baby step for us to take. We shopped for him before we ever got married, and by the time we picked him up last week, he was trained with basic commands. I had been continuing his training at home. I was glad to have him there with me. Buddy made my transition easier. Warren lived a busy lifestyle, maintaining connections in Nashville, and Buddy was my little pal when he wasn't home.

Warren and I were together a lot, but we also had time when we were apart, working on our own things. I knew I would make connections and a life in Nashville, but for now, I was doing my best to adjust to my new life and to being a puppy's stay-at-home mom.

August had come from Memphis for the weekend to stay with Buddy and me while Warren went out of town. Warren would leave tomorrow and be gone for two days. I didn't need my brother to stay with me, I could make it on my own. But the house was big, and I was happy when I ran it past him and he said he could come for a visit. I had grown up being so close to August that I really missed his presence these last couple of months.

He was currently outside in the pool, trying to coax Buddy to go in. I could see him from inside the house. He insisted that Buddy should *love* water on account of him being a retriever, but so far, nothing.

Warren was in Franklin, playing golf with some higher-ups at his record label. He would be busy for the better part of the day. August and I had plans to go to lunch, but he wanted to swim first. I had been outside with him and Buddy, but I went in to use the restroom.

"Stop trying to make him go in," was the first thing I said when I opened the sliding glass door and stepped outside.

August was sitting on the steps of the pool, with his hand out, inviting, coaxing Buddy to the pool. "He'll love it once he gets in," August said. "I'm telling you, we should just pick him up and do it… toss him in… rip it off, like a band-aid. He'll love it once he gets in here."

"We're not ripping any band-aids off of you, little Buddy," I spoke in a dazed cooing tone as I sat down, staring blankly into the pool, past my brother.

A minute passed, and I heard my brother speaking louder.

"See?" he said excitedly. "I told you!"

"You put him in?" I asked incredulously, my gaze snapping that way.

"I've been sitting here telling you to look this way fifty times," August said. "He's swimming!"

"I'm sorry. I'm just… thinking."

"What's wrong? Look at him! Good boy! See? They know how to swim. What's wrong? Why are you in a stare?"

"I'm late."

"For what?"

"My period."

"Oh, girl stuff? Oh, wait, what's that mean?"

"Well, August, I don't know. It could mean something. But we're not planning for that. We just got a dog."

"Are you being serious right now? Are you pregnant, Sasha?"

August was in such shock that he absentmindedly walked out of the pool, holding the dog in front of him, both of them dripping.

"No, no, get back in. You're overreacting. I'm just late."

"What's late?" he asked, setting Buddy down. "I think that means you're pregnant."

Buddy shook, and it was precious. I smiled, but it was tinged with worry. I was never, ever late for my period. Every month, it came a day earlier than it did the last month—maybe I could be off by a day, but today was day four.

"It could just be stress or whatever. I'll probably start tomorrow."

"What stress?" he asked, staring down at me.

I was sitting on a couch, by a pool.

"You know, just traveling or whatever. It could have my system just… different."

August and I got dressed, we put Buddy in his kennel, and left the house. We decided to go by the drugstore on our way to lunch. The plan was to eat some pasta and breadsticks at an Italian restaurant and then I would take the pregnancy test when we got back to the house.

I found two different types at the store, and each box contained two tests. I bought them both, so I had four tests in my possession. I figured that would be enough.

We sat in the waiting area because the restaurant had a ten-minute wait to get a table. The food smelled delicious, and I knew it would taste good, but I wasn't hungry at all.

"What are you thinking about?" August asked.

"What do you think? Can you imagine? What if that happens?"

"Then you would be a great mom, Sasha, obviously."

"We weren't even thinking about children. We just got Buddy. Warren called him 'his son' last night."

"Well, he might have another son soon," August said pointing vaguely at my mid-section. "Where are those tests?" he asked.

"In my bag."

"Go take it."

"Now?"

"Yes. There's a restroom right there."

"I can't do that in a restaurant."

"Why not? Just do it and stick it in your purse when you're done. It would feel good to do it and get it off your mind."

The next thing I knew, I was in a public restroom stall, trying to aim onto the end of a test. It was a little tricky for a first-timer, but I managed.

I had no idea. I put the cap on the test and set it aside while I dealt with my clothing. By the time I picked it up again, there was something on the screen. It was two lines. There were two distinct lines on the screen. I blinked at it. It was a positive result, and I knew it.

I shook as I stuck it in my purse. I washed my hands before heading back into the waiting room.

In my heart, I knew there was a life-changing event happening to me, and I was instantly the most excited I had ever been.

I felt joy indescribable.

I had no idea I wanted to be a mother, and the instant I saw that second line on the test I knew I not only wanted to be one, but I suddenly desperately hoped that it wasn't a false positive.

"Do they show false positives sometimes?" I asked myself, mumbling as I left the restroom.

"What did you say? We got a table," August said, gesturing at me with a come here motion when he saw me come out.

We started walking, following the hostess to our table. I was dazed, and August was anxious to know what happened.

"What did it say? Is it positive?"

I went to my brother, putting my arm around his midsection and holding onto him as we walked, following behind the hostess. I didn't say anything to answer him until we got to the table. He looked at me with an intense expression as soon as the hostess turned her back.

"It says it is, but I know they can be wrong. Can they be wrong?"

"Wait, what are you saying? Did you say 'it says it is'? What's that mean?"

"It says I am, it says we are."

"We are what… having a baby?" he asked slowly, still staring at me.

I nodded stiffly, and August slammed his hands on the table. It wasn't obnoxiously loud, but it surprised me, and I jumped.

"Really? Am I an uncle?"

"Brother, don't."

"Don't what? Are you upset?"

"No, I'm not upset. I'm definitely not upset. I, I just don't know if it's true or not, and I don't want to get my hopes up."

"Did you go in the bathroom and take a test?"

"Yes."

"And does the test say that you're pregnant?"

I took the white stick out of my bag and held it up so that my brother could inspect it. He blinked leaning over the table and staring at it so hard that his eyebrows furrowed.

"That is, clear as day, two lines, Sasha! You're pregnant! I'm gonna be an uncle!"

"What if it's false?"

"They don't go that way. I heard Owen and Shep talking about it. If a test says positive, you're definitely pregnant."

"Really? For sure? I mean it's not like Owen and Shep are the authorities on the subject."

"Other people were there, too. Women. Everyone agreed."

"You had a conversation about pregnancy tests?"

"Yes. I think this means you actually are going to have a baby, Sasha."

I stared at him from across the table. "I have to tell Warren."

***

It was four hours later when Warren got home. I had just finished wiping the counter and was standing in the kitchen. Warren had been golfing, and he had on nice pants with a three-button shirt. It was no longer tucked in, but he looked more dressed up than usual.

"Whatchu doin', bee?"

"I'm wiping the counter. Just from where… my brother made some dinner."

"I thought you were cooking for all of us."

"I got takeout. August already ate and left."

"Are you okay?" he asked the question as he ducked, trying to get me to look at him.

"Oh, yeah, definitely, I'm fine. I just, I wasn't even that hungry, so it was tedious to think about cooking a big meal today."

"What you mean, tedious? Where's August? I thought we were all hanging out here." He peered around our feet, on the floor. "Where's Buddy?"

"He's with August. They went to the park. The Parthenon."

"Centennial?"

"Yes," I agreed.

"That's like an hour from here this time of day."

"I know. He wanted to give us a minute."

"You mean us?" he asked, taking me into his arms. He still smelled nice, even after being out all day. He kissed my neck and I held onto his forearms, gently pressing my fingertips into his skin.

"I have to tell you something," I said. I was nervous, and my voice came out softer than I meant for it to.

"Are you okay, my love?" He pulled off his shirt, stretching upward and wiggling just the right way to pry it off of his body. "I'm going to take a shower," he said, tossing it to the side. "Tell me what you want to tell me, and then I'll go."

I continued to run my fingertips along his arms.

"Why don't you just come in there with me?"

I smiled and took a deep breath. "Hey, you know how we just got Buddy?"

I had no idea where I was going with this. I had all afternoon to think about it. I should have come up with a speech by now.

"Yeah."

"Would it be terrible if we had even more responsibility than that?"

He kissed my neck. "What does that mean? Do you want another dog?"

"No, definitely not."

I didn't know how to say it. I wanted to just come out and tell him that I had taken four pregnancy tests today and they had all confirmed that were having a baby. But I couldn't get any of that news to come out of my mouth.

I looked at him, my sweet, talented, ridiculously gorgeous husband. He was a rebel in so many ways, and yet I felt entirely safe and secure in his care. I wasn't scared of his reaction, it was just that I didn't know how to tell him. Usually, we were good at communication, and I thought I would be able to come out and say it, but I just couldn't.

I had doubts because *what if it turned out not to be true?* But I had taken four tests, and all of them said the same thing.

"Sash, what's going on?"

I didn't say anything. I couldn't.

"What is it?"

I was at such a loss for words that I simply took his hand and manipulated it so that his palm touched my lower abdomen. He pulled it away like he had been electrocuted, but then he gently and instantly put it back.

"Sashaaa," my name came out of his mouth in a hoarse whisper. "Is there a little baby in here?" He put one hand on the front of my stomach and one at the small of my back, holding me in place.

"Warren, are we ready for this?"

"Is there a baby?"

"Yes."

"Then we're ready."

"Really?"

"Yesssss. Are you serious right now?" His smile was so big, it lit up his whole face. His instant excitement lifted actual weight off of my shoulders. "Did you take a pregnancy test?"

"Yes."

"And it said we are?"

"Yes."

He let go of my mid-section, and repositioned himself, holding me, taking me into his arms. I looked up at him, and he kissed me. I had been intimidated by the thought of what he'd say, and the relief of his approval made the whole kiss taste like sweet honey. He opened his mouth to me, and I felt loved, desired, accepted, and protected.

He pulled back, staring at me. "Are you happy?"

I nodded. "I am. Especially now that you're happy."

"Sasha, I am the most happy. I can't believe this. Are you sure? Are we having a baby?"

I nodded, and Warren looked up and let out a loud whistle. He knew how to do it really loud, and I laughed and held my ears.

We would spend the rest of the night in a couple's utopia, holding onto each other and making plans for our baby—and we would spend the rest of our lives loving each other and loving him.

The End

(till book 3)

Thanks to my team ~ Chris, Coda, Skye, Jan, Glenda, and Yvette

Made in the USA
Columbia, SC
22 May 2025

58286377R10133